# The SECRET of the POINTED TOWER

## PIERRE VÉRY

Translated from the French by Tom Mead
Introduction by Tom Mead

# The
# SECRET of the
# POINTED
# TOWER

## PIERRE VÉRY

Translated from the French by Tom Mead
Introduction by Tom Mead

CRIPPEN & LANDRU PUBLISHERS
Cincinnati, Ohio
2024

## ELLERY QUEEN'S MYSTERY MAGAZINE

An American Mercury Publication. ~~570 Lexington Avenue, New York 22, N.Y.~~

Lawrence E. Spivak, PUBLISHER. Ellery Queen, EDITOR

July 26, 1948

Dear Pierre Véry,

"Q"

I cannot tell you how grateful I am to you, for sending me one of your own copies of LES VEILLÉES DE LA TOUR POINTUE, and for inscribing it to me. I have known of this book for a long time, but have never been able to find a copy.

I do not read French well, but I will have someone I trust read the book for me — with a view to my writing you again about the possibility of reprinting some of the stories in my magazine. At the proper time I shall discuss fees, rights, and so on.

I am taking the liberty of sending you a copy of my ~~last~~ latest anthology. I hope you read English better than I do French — I am

(over)

anxious to have your opinion of Queen's Quorum — the first attempt ever to do this sort of thing.

Again, my deepest thanks to you for your kindness. Your book is now one of the treasures in my collection.

Sincerely,

Frederic Dannay
(Ellery Queen)
29 Byron Lane
Larchmont, New York

For information contact:
Crippen & Landru, Publishers
P. O. Box 532057
Cincinnati, OH 45253 USA

Web: www.crippenlandru.com
E-mail: Orders@crippenlandru.com

ISBN (softcover): 978-1-936363-81-0
ISBN (clothbound): 978-1-936363-82-7


First Edition: December 2023

10  9  8  7  6  5  4  3  2  1

# Contents

# INTRODUCTION

## By Tom Mead

Later in life, Pierre Véry would claim he had received two pieces of particular good fortune in his youth. "First, to have lived my first twelve years in the countryside, and second, to have had no money." The former taught him about the world, while the latter taught him about life. He would put these formative experiences to great use when he discovered his true vocation as a master of the *roman policier.*

Pierre was born on November 17th, 1900, at Couret farm in Bellon, near Aubeterre-sur-Dronne in south-western France. His parents were Jean and Lucie (née Pigeaud). As a child, he was an avid reader of tales by the likes of Jules Verne and Thomas Mayne Reid, which helped to stimulate his own thirst for adventure. His mother also nurtured his imagination by regaling him with legends and folklore of the region. Those legends, as well as the rural, agrarian lifestyle of Charente, held great personal significance throughout his life, which was reflected in his work.

But Lucie Véry died when she was only 39; Pierre was 13. Less than three years later, in 1916, the Véry family would be struck by tragedy again when Pierre's brother Jean-Camille was killed in the Great War at the age of 22. Jean-Camille was six years Pierre's senior, and his only sibling.

Subsequently, Pierre commenced (and swiftly abandoned) seminary studies, before serving briefly in the military himself in 1920. He worked a string of menial occupations during this period of poverty that he would eventually look back on with fondness. Among his many professions were bicycle courier, kitchen assistant on a cargo ship, and assistant at a book store. And all the while he harboured an insatiable desire for travel and adventure, which he finally indulged when he and his friend Pierre Béarn made an ill-advised attempt to circumnavigate the globe. By 1924, though, he had settled in Paris and was running his own bookshop: the *Galerie du Zodiaque.*

In the following years, Pierre began to write short fiction and articles under a variety of pseudonyms, and before the end of the decade he had completed his first novel: *Pont-Égaré* was published in 1929. It is a work of considerable merit; a kind of magical-realist fable set in Charente, the rural landscape of his youth.

It was a finalist for the prestigious Prix Goncourt, presaging its author's rapid rise to stardom in the literary world. However, in spite of critical acclaim, neither *Pont-Égaré* nor Pierre's next work, *Danse a l'ombre*, became a bestseller or yielded much in the way of financial success, though they were championed by— among others—Andre Malraux.

It was a foray into the mystery genre that saw Pierre's first tangible commercial hit. Winner of the *Prix du Roman d'Aventures* in 1930, *The Testament of Basil Crookes* was described by *L'Ordre* as "a joyous cocktail of humor and adventure" (October 10th, 1930). But this placed its author in a somewhat awkward position—he found himself torn between his literary ambition and his commercial inclinations. This, in turn, led him to forge his own unique path through the Golden Age of Detective Fiction.

In some respects, Pierre Véry enjoys the distinction of being both an exponent and a critic of the Golden Age. He tells mysterious tales, and yet these tales often exist outside of the strict parameters of the conventional whodunit. Some are subversive reimaginings, while others are conscious parodies, but they are all plotted and written with the meticulousness and respect for the genre that we have come to expect of our Golden Age greats. What set his work apart from that of his contemporaries was his often-eccentric blending of genres, and his taste for the surreal or fantastical.

He was also remarkably prolific, with not one but five novels appearing under his name in 1934. Among them was the superb *Les quatre vipères*, and *Meurtre Quai des Orfèvres*, in which he introduced his longest-running series detective: the lawyer and amateur sleuth Prosper Lepicq.

Hitting his stride, Véry penned seven Lepicq novels between 1934 and 1937, seven additional crime novels, plus a collection of short stories—this collection of short stories, in fact. The mysterious, challenging, beguiling, never-short-of-fascinating tales which comprise this collection, *The Secret of the Pointed Tower.*

What makes these stories so successful is Véry's unwillingness to be bound by convention. It's not only that; his stories engage actively with many of the themes and motifs which are familiar to us as readers of mystery fiction. But it is his handling of those themes and motifs which demonstrates his true artistry. By turns irreverent and innovative, this collection sets out to reinterpret and subvert at each turn. In this respect, Pierre

Véry was an author ahead of his time. Indeed, this collection (which has never before appeared in English), is certainly ripe for critical reappraisal—as are the author's novels.

The framework narrative sees Véry himself walking the streets of Paris in search of the perfect setting for his next murder mystery. His wanderings take him past the eponymous "pointed tower," *La Tour Pointue,* which is part of the famous police headquarters on the Quai des Orfèvres. It then transpires that this location—familiar to readers from countless French crime novels—is harbouring a most unusual secret. Véry is merely the amanuensis, he assures us, and every tale he is about to tell is completely and entirely true. It's that sort of playfulness which distinguishes his work from the more staid and prosaic efforts of some of his contemporaries.

In an interview with La Liberte which appeared on February 7th, 1934, Véry placed himself in direct opposition to the likes of Georges Simenon, who imbued the *roman policier* with a sense of gritty realism, and was an early exponent of what we would now call the "police procedural" subgenre. "I try to introduce as much fantasy as I can, unlike Simenon," says Véry, going on to observe: "For me, the roman policier is the brother of the fairy tale."

These tales are bizarre – baroque, if you prefer—albeit without the uncanny malevolence of, for example, Boileau-Narcejac's *D'Entre les morts.* One cannot help but imagine that Véry's tongue is wedged firmly in cheek throughout. This adds to their charm. For instance, "The Tale of a Tartlet" is a kind of anti-murder mystery: our protagonist knows he has killed someone—but who? Then there is "The Mystery of the Green Room," which is playfully (and meta-textually) described as an "*un*-locked-room mystery."

But as well as entertainments, the stories are social documents of great historical interest. They reflect not only the mores and conventions of their time, but also the jokes, the cultural references and allusions, the day-to-day preoccupations. Each is a microcosm of French life in the years before the outbreak of the Second World War.

Another aspect of Véry's talent that shines through in this collection is his sheer literariness. That is to say, his eye for detail, his knack for crafting memorable, distinctive characters, his lyrical descriptiveness, his colourful lexicon, and overall the sheer quality of his prose. It is hard not to be swept away by these audacious flights of fancy. A 1941 review of *L'Assassinat du Père Noel*, a film adaptation of one of his novels, praises the director for capturing the "poetry" that Véry brings to the detective novel. Read *The Secret of the Pointed Tower*, the reviewer advises, and "you will have a fair idea of how Véry transforms a detective plot into a fantastic, magical and charming tale" (*Compagnons*, November 8th, 1941). I am inclined to agree.

It's fair to say that when *The Secret of the Pointed Tower* was published in its original French, it was met with widespread critical acclaim. "The critics who have championed Pierre Véry from the beginning agree that he has breathed new life into the 'detective novel,'" said *Les Nouvelles Litteraires* (August 14th, 1937). "Pierre Véry is the best contemporary detective novelist," said *Arts & idees* (December 1st, 1937). "Here is humor at its finest," said *Le Peuple* (September 1st, 1937).

Bearing in mind its resoundingly positive reception, it is perhaps surprising that the book has never before been translated into English. Indeed, its reputation certainly reached the Anglophone world, with Ellery Queen's excellent Queen's Quorum (1951) favoring the book with more than a passing mention. It is (rightly) described as "a volume of short stories held in high esteem by French critics" (p.95) in a section which also neatly captures the contradictory nature of Véry 's work as a whole. Queen cites his "passion for realism" which manifests in his acute eye for detail, coupled with "the lure of romance" epitomized by his more colorful flights of fancy. As evidence, the inimitable EQ cites perhaps the most outlandish title in this collection: "The 700,000 Pink Radishes."

Indeed, perhaps it is this offbeat sensibility which has made the collection such a challenge; it is, after all, difficult to categorize these stories. Some are comic, some are thrilling, some are disturbing. And yet they are all pure Véry. Each tale offers something that is unique, eccentric, and incredibly rewarding: the opportunity to escape to a more whimsical world. If that isn't worth the investment of a reader's time, I don't know what is.

Pierre Véry's unorthodox brand of storytelling turned him into a literary celebrity in France. As well as his novels, he had a very lucrative sideline as a screenwriter. Beginning with the gritty, uncompromising *L'Enfer des anges* in 1939, he collaborated on twenty-one scripts, including the film adaptation of his own novel, *Les Anciens de Saint-Loup*, in 1950. There were also eight other adaptations of his work during his lifetime.

So it's fair to say that when he gave an interview to *Cine-mondial* (published October 24th, 1941), he was a man at the peak of his creative powers. He took that opportunity to reminisce about his youth, and to make the remark about the two pieces of good fortune which began this introduction. When quizzed on his writing process, Véry pointed out that there were no "recettes spéciales," or secret recipes. Ideas were typically stimulated by "a title, a character, or a location." The article also noted that "[h]e now lives in a modern building in the heart of Grenelle [a neighborhood in Paris], not far from the rue du Commerce where the bustling produce market is also for Pierre Véry a character market."

Véry was a married man by this time; he wed Jeanne Rouvin in 1939, and the couple would have three children together: Madeline, Dominique, and Noel. He remained prolific throughout the Nazi Occupation of France, but by the end of the Second World War he had grown disaffected with the crime genre, and yearned to pursue the loftier literary ambitions of his early days. In an interview with *Le Litteraire* (October 19th, 1946), he renounced crime fiction altogether. "I've never written crime novels," he claimed. "At most two of my books deserve that description. As for the others, let's call them 'mystery stories.'" In that interview, he put forward a deceptively simple creative philosophy: "Basically," he concluded, "I am looking for means of escape from a world that does not particularly interest me."

So, was his renouncement of mystery fiction to be permanent or temporary? "Permanent," came the answer. "I'll write three or four more books which I've signed up for, and that will be it."

In the final decade of his life Pierre Véry produced three novels, but seemed more dedicated to the silver screen; he worked on eleven screenplays with a revolving roster of collaborators. He died suddenly in 1960, at the age of 59, cutting short a truly remarkable career which has left an indelible mark on French culture.

More recent assessments of his work have endeavored to analyze their unorthodox ingredients. For instance, in his chapter on Véry in *Mythologie du roman policier*, Francis Lacassin provides an in-depth critical appraisal of his oeuvre, highlighting its preoccupation with the unusual; the dream-like. Aptly enough, the chapter is titled "The Police in the Land of the Fairies."

Among the many insightful observations in Lacassin's critique is the importance of the mise-en-scène. The "ghostly transformation" of the countryside by "the wind, the nocturnal sounds, the moon." This is a particularly prominent feature of *The Secret of the Pointed Tower*, where Véry brings a lyrical sensibility to his depictions of both rural and urban settings.

In *Lire le roman policier*, meanwhile, Franck Evrard draws a neat correlation between Véry and Lewis Carroll. Through the medium of the detective story, Véry reconciles death and madness, imbuing the former with poetry and the latter with its own internal logic. The logic of dreams, if you like, which manifests as a form of magical realism.

The Golden Age of mystery and detective fiction seems to be enjoying a popular resurgence in recent years, with many forgotten and neglected authors coming back into print and, in some cases, enjoying larger readerships than they ever did in their lifetimes. Additionally, authors of that era whose works have never before been translated are finally finding fame among English-speaking readers. Prominent examples include the Japanese honkaku mystery writers Seishi Yokomizo and Tetsuya Ayakawa, as well as Frenchmen Noel Vindry and Boileau-Narcejac. I'm delighted that we can now add Pierre Véry to that ever-lengthening list. He is undeniably an important figure in the evolution of the French mystery story; one whose creativity and ambition imbued his work with a sense of what *L'Ordre* termed "the secret magic" at the heart of things.

### A Note on La Tour Pointue

La Tour Pointue still stands at 36, Quai des Orfèvres, on the Left Bank of the River Seine. However, the building no longer serves as headquarters for the Police Judiciaire—the PJ relocated to its new home on the rue de Bastion, near the Porte de Clichy, in July 2017. But the pointed tower remains a potent symbol of law and justice, as well as an imposing silhouette on the Paris skyline.

### A Note on The Mystery of the Yellow Room

A warning to anyone who has not yet read Gaston Leroux's

1907 mystery classic, *The Mystery of the Yellow Room*: the novel features prominently in not one but two of the stories included here, namely "The Mystery of the Green Room" and "A Lesson in Crime." In both instances, the identity of the murderer is discussed at length.

*Tom Mead is a UK-based author and Golden Age aficionado. His debut novel,* Death and the Conjuror, *was an international bestseller, and named one of the best mysteries of 2022 by* Publishers Weekly. *The sequel,* The Murder Wheel, *was published in July 2023, and described as "compelling" by Crimereads and "pure nostalgic pleasure" by the* Wall Street Journal. *His short fiction has appeared in* Ellery Queen's Mystery Magazine, Alfred Hitchcock Mystery Magazine, *and* The Best Mystery Stories of the Year, *edited by Lee Child.*

Tom Mead
August 2023

# A MESSAGE TO
# THE READER

(in confidence)

Dearest reader and friend, of course you are familiar with the Police Judiciaire HQ at *Quai des Orfèvres*– a building colloquially known as *la Tour Pointue*—the Pointed Tower. You know it well. You have climbed its shabby yet somewhat forbidding staircase. You have visited each of its dark, dusty rooms before (for curiosity's sake, of course!).

But do you know "the mousetrap"?

Not far from "the lion's den," the guardroom where officers wear out their fingers playing cards; not far from the infirmary, where the sound of nuns at evening prayer hums like a beehive; at the very end of the courtyard, near the kitchens, you will find the mousetrap. This underground passage serves as a short cut from *la Cour du Dépôt* —oft-frequented by ladies of the night— to *la Cour de la Sainte-Chapelle*.

Do you like secret passages, dear reader? Personally, I love them. They evince a delicious frisson, and from time to time yield wonders.

Thus, one evening I headed down this damp tunnel. That morning I had just poisoned two innocent young girls with cyanide and slit the throat of a defenseless old man. But I had to kill again. My reserve of poison was exhausted and I found the copious bloodshed somewhat distasteful: Who would have thought the old man to have had so much blood in him, as they say?

In short, I was looking for somewhere to hang a man—just to spice things up a little.

Such is the morbid fate of mystery writers: they must search relentlessly throughout the city, the suburbs, even overseas, for places to commit the most heinous of crimes and have a decent chance of getting away with them. They take careful note of these places, as others might take note of underground cafés, or cinemas with discreet, screened boxes. Crime scenes are their "stomping ground." In confidence they say things to each other like: "If you want to gut that pensioner of yours and get away with it, I'd recommend *l'impasse des Essards,* in the *xvième arrondissement.* A hundred percent private. Now, in return, can you think of a decent spot to kidnap a scientist who's just perfected an invention of vital interest to national security?"

But let us return to the mousetrap.

I was alone. The tunnel was dimly lit by a single bulb. Overhead was a circular air vent, covered by an iron grille. The place seemed perfect for the crime I had in mind.

Even the proximity of the police suited the crime—it added a hint of danger. The man I intended to hang being of average build, I summoned all my strength and jumped up to grab hold of the grille, to check it could carry my weight. Needless to say, I am a stickler for detail. But I lost my grip and, as I tumbled, smacked my back against the wall which is on the left as you walk towards *la cour du Dépôt.* I fell backward.

Backward!

*Through* the wall!

I quickly realized this phenomenon, though disturbing, was in no way supernatural. In fact, the wall had moved.

By a marvelous coincidence, my shoulder had triggered some sort of invisible secret button, which caused an aperture in the wall to open. I was now lying on my back in a narrow passage where even a child would struggle to stand upright.

Dearest reader, imagine my surprise! But my profession as an author has taught me how to handle such occurrences. I quickly regained my composure and resolved to show as much courage as my heroes did upon finding themselves in similar situations.

I closed the secret door behind me, having studied the mechanism and assured myself I would be able to get out again when I needed to.

I ignited my lighter—the cheap sort you might win at a fairground—and began to crawl. It was exhausting. Extremely uncomfortable, not to mention grotesque. It occurred to me how cruel I had been in forcing some of my fictional heroes to do the very same thing. Nevertheless, my fascination kept me going. Besides, scarcely seven or eight minutes of crawling led me to the foot of a staircase so narrow that I could only enter it at an angle.

I counted ninety-three steps: approximately five floors up.

At the very top I found a padlocked door, which I tackled like a professional.

I entered a round, airless room which was so stuffy I could hardly breathe. I opened a mullioned window, leaned out and caught sight of the Seine. I was at the very top of *la Tour Pointue*.

*Shame*, I said to myself, *there's no moon tonight*. I could scarcely make out a thing in that darkened room. And at that moment, as if by magic, a full moon emerged from between the clouds.

There was no furniture, save for a table and chair. But, on the table, lining the walls, on the floor, in sheaves, in piles, in heaps; bound in green, red, yellow, blue, gray folders; held together with straps, strings, clips, rubber bands; were files positively crammed with papers.

I picked up a bundle and undid the strap. It contained seven files, numbered in red ink, each one bearing an unusual title: "The Affair of the Four Watches," "The Talking Ghost of Talafeix," "The 700,000 Pink Radishes," "The Kidnapped Clergyman," "The Strange Vision of Miss Dorothee F. Bridge," "The Spanish Prisoner," "The Tale of a Tartlet."

What sort of police archive was this?

Some reports were recorded in extraordinarily fine and ornate handwriting; others in plain, bold script. I deduced that the first author was a miser, the second a more prodigal, playful sort.

These reports contained all kinds of crimes, burglaries, mysteries, enigmas. Oddly enough, though, they were not like any other police reports I had ever seen: dry, precise, clinical. These were stories, with (at least on the part of the man with large handwriting), a cynical sense of humor.

Often, they detailed swindles, larcenies and other puzzles with scant police involvement. How, then, had the men in *la Tour Pointue* heard about them? And why had they not been made public?

I told myself that the police, who know practically everything, only tell the public what they want them to know. In other words, almost nothing.

In any case, for a writer like me, what a godsend!

All I had to do was copy them word for word, without changing a single comma. Naturally I could not actually remove them, so I would copy them. I would return each night to continue my work as a clandestine copyist at the top of *la Tour Pointue*.

Overcome by my discovery, I leaned against the window frame for a moment. I briefly contemplated the Seine; those waters positively viscous with the filth and debris of so many liquefied corpses. So many secrets. Then I made an effort to imagine what these two extravagant archivists looked like. I decided that one was sallow, uptight, with an unappealing squint; the other somewhat paunchy, robust, with the build of an ox, the face of an ox and (unfortunately) the breath of one, too. The first man favored pinches of snuff; the second rolled fat cigarettes. The first, wearing white gloves and a tasseled cap on his bald head, wrote with a pen nib as sharp as a thorn; the second, shirt sleeves rolled up, veins the size of earthworms writhing on his forearm, scribbled his reports with a goose feather quill, enthusiastically flicking ink in all directions.

A clock striking midnight across the *boulevard du Palais* brought me back to reality.

Notebook. Pen.

Ignoring the thousand Buridans pursuing their thousand Marguerites across the sleeping city, heedless of the world beyond the window, I wrote feverishly.

In shorthand, I copied the contents of one folder, then another. The hours rolled by. Sometimes, to give my aching fingers a rest, I paused and gazed at my surroundings: it was a look charged with the covetousness of Ali Baba in the cave of the forty thieves, with the treasures heaped up around him, lamenting that he would never be able to carry them all.

Only at dawn did my vigil in *la Tour Pointue* come to an end.

Today, dearest reader, I offer you the spoils of this vigil. Don't blame me if you find it somewhat jumbled. That's not my fault. Remember, I didn't have time to sift through it all. I saw my chance and I took it. As luck would have it, most of the reports I copied were written by the paunchy and jovial archivist.

Take the first one, for instance. It was somewhat cumbersomely titled: "Criminal Investigation Course," and numbered 7.888.419.G.J. I confess that I did not quite grasp the meaning or significance of this designation. I copied it, however, as a curiosity.

All the same, it was written in the hand of the paunchy, jovial archivist.

# URBIN'S CHIN

I suppose the only reason I stayed behind in that house is that I was afraid. Yes, it was a stubborn reaction against the idiotic sense of dread which tapped me on the shoulder, sent shivers up my spine and whistled a little ditty in my ear; a song about the pure, clean air of the place des Abbesses, at the other end of Paris—where I lived.

Admittedly, my fear was unreasonable. But that evening also marked my very first adventure. I was new to this particular "vocation," and I suppose even the most experienced burglars can look back on their debuts and recall the same sort of anguish that I felt that night.

While I'm at it, let me introduce myself. I am Simonet, also known as "the book-taker," specialist in the theft of rare tomes. I'm thirty years of age. I am not particularly tall, or handsome, or strong. But I have three other things going for me. First: my cunning. I have a splendidly well-organized brain, like a filing cabinet with all sorts of secret compartments. That's where I keep all my tricks. Second: I am a bibliophile. From the beginning of the sixteenth century to the end of the seventeenth, I know all there is to know about books. I'm a walking encyclopedia. I could make a decent living as a bookseller if I put my mind to it. And third: though I'm not what you could call robust, I *do* have excellent legs. That means I can reach impressive speeds when I have to. But I hasten to add that this particular skill was of no use to me whatsoever during the affair of Urbin's chin. There was no opportunity to demonstrate my athletic prowess.

I was well-prepared. I had settled in an abandoned construction site dressed as a tramp, and spent close to a week studying the comings and goings of this quaint little cul-de-sac, lined with rosebushes, which nestled at the end of the *xivème* arrondissement. It was August. Most of the residents were at the seaside or in the country—all except for Urbin. He was the man I was watching. Tucked away in his library was a renowned collection of literary rarities. As you can imagine, I had my heart set on acquiring some of the choicest titles.

I had already observed that Urbin—a short man in his sixties, who dressed in an old-fashioned manner; jacket, bowler hat, polished boots; and had the air of a retired professor about him—lived alone. An unsentimental woman with all the charm of a bag of nails did his housework and cooked his meals, then went home. Also, a large hulking gardener usually worked on the property from nine in the morning until around six in the afternoon. Ostensibly, he was gardening. But in fact he spent most of his time leaning on the handle of his shovel—which was firmly stuck in the hard ground, before collapsing into his wheelbarrow in exhaustion. Then he slept like Hercules must have slept after completing his twelve labors. This Hercules, however, was not too keen on labor of any kind.

Every afternoon—apart from Sunday—Urbin trotted over to the Latin Quarter, a veritable paradise of booksellers. Invariably, his wandering brought him to the docks. He usually headed along Rue Mazarine at around seven o'clock, then ducked into a modest meat-and-potatoes sort of restaurant. He dined, paying less attention to his meal than to whichever book he happened to be leafing through, with a tenderness I knew all too well. He left the restaurant at around half-past eight, then pressed on toward Chatelet. There, he sometimes struck lucky and found what he was looking for straight away—or sometimes not. In such instances, he remained patient, pacing slowly up and down the street. What he was looking for was a cab. *His* cab. At that time—1920—there were hardly any cabs left in Paris, so he did not have much choice. The carriage itself was run-down, and the horse decidedly past its prime. The coachman was equally indecorous, with a long, ragged red beard protruding from his chin in all directions like a wild bush. Florid features, beady eyes beneath the brim of his hat, a bulbous nose. He reminded me instantly of a caricature I had seen in the Trombinoscope: this coachman looked like Paul Verlaine.

And as soon as he spotted old Urbin, he approached with a crack of his whip and a grunted greeting.

Urbin settled himself in the carriage, and they were on their way back toward the impasse aux Rosiers, reaching home at around ten o'clock.

That night, I approached the house at a little after seven.

Not too early, not too late. Good. Everything so far had gone off without a hitch. My marmoset had gently opened the gate for me, then the door. Very nice. No one about, not even a cat. I made for the library and selected a handful of titles. No more than twenty, but enough to yield a decent profit—I had a client in Chicago who was willing to pay handsomely. Perfect. No fingerprints, no mess, no trace of my presence other than a few discreet gaps in the shelves. In short, an excellent start. In the hallway, I piled the books on top of an old wooden chest and bound them together with a strap.

But then I was struck by this sudden fit of fear. Utterly without cause—it was not even nine o'clock yet. A simple matter of nerves. I felt a fool. To scuttle away from the house at that point would have felt... wrong, somehow. So, in order to toughen myself up a little, I decided to stick around for a while. I headed up to the first floor, even though I had no business up there, and began to poke around in the bedroom. On the mantel, a clock struck nine.

At that moment, the cobbled street beyond the window resounded with the squeak of wheels and the clatter of hooves. What was this? That tired old horse, dragging the run-down carriage already? Could it be? I ran to the window. Unfortunately, the branches of a chestnut tree in the garden blocked my view.

But I did not need to see it. I had been listening to it for a week; the sound of that horse was etched into my brain. I knew it well.

When the carriage drew up in front of the house, I caught a glimpse of the coachman's gibus. Then I heard the sound of voices; I could make out Urbin's. I ducked away from the window. The gate creaked, I heard footsteps on the path, then the front door opened downstairs.

Now, abject terror clung to me like a cold sweat. My shirt stuck to my back, then peeled away like a blister as I moved. I darted around the place like a rat on the run from a bloodthirsty feline. I was ashamed of myself. Finally, I calmed down sufficiently to realize it would be advantageous to find a hiding place. I slithered under the bed. Then I heard the echoes of a conversation downstairs, but could not make out what was said. I did, however, make out the coachman's voice: "Have a good evening, ladies and gents," he said. Then came the clatter of hooves once more, receding into silence. The coachman was gone.

About half an hour passed. I remained in my hiding place, watching and listening. But no matter how much I tried, I still could not make out a word. Only from time to time a strange creaking, like an old rocking chair.

I stayed under the bed for as long as I could. But soon, cramp was slithering up my left leg like a colony of ants. The occasional spider or cockroach approached across the floor, and when they ventured too close I sent them skittering away by blowing on them. Finally, I could stand it no longer; I crawled out of my hiding place.

I took the stairs, moving silently on my crepe soles.

In the hallway below, there was not a trace of Urbin. Nor his guests. Nor a single flicker of light. I did not hang around to ponder this—I was itching to get away, and the horrible urge to make a run for it left me hopping anxiously from foot to foot. In the darkness, I reached out to grab my parcel from the top of the wooden trunk. It was gone. For a moment I slid my fingers over the smooth surface of the trunk—they came away sticky. I sniffed them, but they smelt of nothing at all. A kind of bland scent, if you like. I switched on my flashlight and lifted the lid of the trunk.

Curled up in the crate, with his head tilted back, was Urbin. His head had been smashed in. His face and jacket were covered in blood and slivers of brain.

I turned off my flashlight. I no longer knew what I was doing. It was the first time I had seen a dead body, and what a sight it was.... I could not breathe. I felt as if my throat had seized up.

At that moment, the front door yawned noiselessly open.

Standing on the threshold was the Herculean gardener. He looked at me with an air of profound bewilderment. He held in his hand a large hammer, stained with crimson spatter. His face quivered. I stared at him, feeling as though I would never stop shaking.

Then, suddenly, the gardener began to scream.

The police who interrogated me were not the surly kind. If they hit me at all, I got the feeling it was merely a formality. A way of honoring an old tradition. But they nonetheless peppered me with questions:

"We know it was you. You might as well confess. Come on,

admit it! You went there to burgle the place, the owner surprised you, so you lashed out! You panicked, it's perfectly understandable, we've seen it a thousand times before. No premeditation. Be sensible, own up. You were caught in the act, so why deny it? You killed him, and then you threw the weapon out into the garden. But what about the wallet? What did you do with Urbin's wallet?"

I told them everything. How I had spied on Urbin and learned his routine, how he usually came home at around ten o'clock. I did not conceal the fact that I had gone there to steal. I explained that he had returned earlier than usual, accompanied by at least one other person. I described the coachman, and my encounter with the gardener, swinging the bloody hammer. When the police got tired of interrogating me, they ordered me back to my cell. On my way out, I heard one of them say: "It can't be *him*. He's too stupid."

"Don't be so sure," retorted the commissioner. "For a moron, he's surprisingly observant."

Though this answer worried me, I don't deny that I also found it strangely satisfying. The commissioner was no fool. Then, I was shoved back into my cell which—truth be told— was fairly clean.

I began to run through the problem once more in my mind. To my mind, there were at least five suspects.

First, the visitor, or *visitors*, who had got out of the carriage with Urbin. But was it a woman alone, or a woman and a man? I was inclined to believe the latter; it must have been the man who delivered the coup de grace. A woman could not have swung the hammer with such force.

The coachman? Unlikely. When could he have done the deed? Unless of course he was in league with Urbin's guests...

The cook? Even less likely.

Lastly, the gardener? Hercules had told the police he returned to the property to check the lock on the greenhouse located behind the main house. He had found the bloody hammer on the garden path, then spotted my flashlight and gone to investigate—that's what he claimed. However, knowing how hard Hercules worked during the daylight hours, I found it difficult to imagine him returning at nine in the evening.

Nevertheless, I could not be sure. I despaired, knowing that my liberty and perhaps my life depended on it.

I slept badly, and woke at dawn in a deep depression. I found out later that the newspapers had already printed a full account of the incident, derived from the gardener's statement and from my own. The coachman's "Have a good evening, ladies and gents," took on extra significance in the gossip columns, and there was much speculation about who Urbin's companions might have been.

Around noon, they took me in for a fresh interrogation. I knew nothing would come of it. And of course, nothing did. They told me they were going to bring in the coachman, who had voluntarily come forward. Soon he appeared. I was struck by just how closely he resembled Paul Verlaine—even more so up close.

I learned that his statement more or less corresponded with mine. Apparently when he picked up Urbin, the old man was not alone. He had two people with him—a man and a woman. They did not seem particularly close friends. The tone of their conversation was oddly formal, he claimed. "At least, that's how it sounded to me," he added.

When they reached Urbin's house, the old man had headed inside to fetch some money for the fare. That was the last time the coachman saw him. He could give only a vague description of the woman: tall, slim, elegant, aged somewhere between twenty-five and thirty. A blonde or brunette, he couldn't really tell. As for the color of her clothes, they had appeared to his untrained eye to be brown.

On the other hand, he was able to give a remarkably precise description of the man who had accompanied Urbin. This was easily explained: the fellow was unique in that, save for one single detail, he was the precise opposite of Urbin. He was tall, broad, and sharply dressed. Urbin was short, puny, and old-fashioned in appearance. The stranger was around forty; Urbin was sixty. The stranger was clean-shaven; Urbin had a moustache. The stranger's face was smooth; Urbin's was wrinkled. But they had one feature and one feature alone in common: the chin.

Urbin was afflicted with a monstrous, protuberant, and quite disproportionate underbite. But the stranger, who differed from Urbin in every other respect, had the same underbite. This detail had not been lost on the coachman. He gave a colorful description of this pair of identical chins. You might even call it passionate; he spoke with a kind of awestruck horror. Donkey jaw, he called it.

Though I was stuck in my cell, I now felt considerably more confident about the outcome of the case. The killer was the man with the donkey jaw, that much was obvious, and the woman was his accomplice. No doubt this would be clear to the authorities, and soon they would see sense and release me. After all, it was only my first offence, and I had not actually managed to steal anything. Above all, I was a polite and obliging prisoner.

Unfortunately for me, the extensive manhunt turned up nothing. In the end, and under considerable pressure from the newspapers, the investigators decided that Urbin's elusive "companions" were pure invention, and that the coachman and myself were accomplices—one man acting as lookout, the other doing the wicked deed.

As you can imagine, I continued to probe the problem from the comfort of my cell, using the only investigative tool at my disposal: my brain. I studied the problem logically. The gardener, the coachman, the cook; the tall, slim, elegant woman of thirty; or this strange man who was so different from Urbin in every aspect save the chin. Which of them was guilty?

The chins... that pair of "donkey jaws"...

No matter how I racked my brains for the solution, I came up with precisely nothing. Eventually, though, an idea began to take shape. A glimmer of light in the darkness. It drew on distinctly flawed and risky reasoning... but reasoning nonetheless. All the same, that greeting made by the coachman—"Have a good evening, ladies and gents!"—was a problem.

And the police remained as ineffectual as ever.

I spent many hours deliberating whether or not to let them in on my hypothesis, but in the end I opted to remain silent. Apart from the fact that the idea of becoming some kind of police informant was not particularly germane given my chosen occupation, I realized that by keeping quiet I might just be able to turn a decent profit out of this. *If*, that is, I ever regained my freedom.

Besides, there was no rush. I could always spill the beans once I had proven my theory correct.

Fortunately, I did not have to wait too long. One by one, the police and the local magistrates grew increasingly frustrated with the problem. They had me in their custody, but it was impossible to prove their case. And so, after three months behind bars,

I suddenly found myself deposited on a Parisian pavement one miserable December morning, a free man.

First, I made a point of seeing the gardener again. I interrogated him—after a fashion, anyway. All it took was a bottle or two. When he told me that there was not only a greenhouse but a *trapdoor leading to the wine cellar* situated in the garden behind the house, I knew at once why he had returned under cover of darkness on the night of the murder.

I asked around about the coachman who looked like Paul Verlaine, and it didn't take long to track him down. I was pleased to hear that—like myself—he had recently been released from custody. Like me, he'd been incarcerated while the investigation was underway. He had taken up his run-down cab and decrepit horse once more, and resumed his daily activities. The unfortunate fellow housed his cab and horse in a stable with a broken lock. Judging from a bunk in the far corner, it looked as though he slept there.

One morning, I decided to follow him. I was not quite sure how to approach the situation, since it was his "Have a good evening, ladies and gents" which had thrown off all my calculations. So I followed the cab. I proceeded on foot, but there was no need to worry about losing sight of him. His half-dead horse trotted as though it were leading a funeral procession. The driver sat motionless, nodding his head slightly, as though he were napping. In fact, he was scarcely driving the cab at all—the horse was panting furiously, and frequently stumbled on the cobbles. It was a pitiful sight. With my overcoat collar around my ears, I followed this pathetic pair of creatures, unable to escape the depressing feeling that I was wasting my time. And all because of that single sentence: "Have a good evening, ladies and gents!"

At place de la République, I was tempted to abandon this pointless pursuit. But, in deference to my own very subtle reasoning, and the conclusion I had reached in my cell, I decided to continue. To take my last chance. I hailed the cab and clambered into the back, shouting "Place Blanche!" as though I were simply saying place Victor Hugo, or Gare d'Orsay. Why did I do this? Even now, I can't tell you. I simply sat, withdrawn and sullen, in the back of the cab. Something inside me whispered *The solution is here... it's here... all you have to do is look, and you'll find it...* At the same time, another voice murmured *What's the use? There's nothing to understand—all he said was "Have a good evening, ladies and gents..."*

At place Blanche I got out and paid the fare. I was no closer to a solution. Feeling disappointed and disoriented, I entered a little bar which was nearly deserted. Behind the bar, the landlord was busy fiddling with the taps of his beer engine—which was apparently out of order—all the while listening with visible frustration to the advice that an off-duty workman with an empty glass insisted on giving him. Finally, the landlord could take it no more so he lifted a hatch and disappeared into the cellar.

The workman left. And at that moment, the light dawned. You see, on his way out of the bar he said, "Have a good evening, ladies and gents." But I was the only one in the bar. *Have a good evening, ladies and gents.* Fool that I was, it had not occurred to me before then that that particular phrase simply rolled off the tongue of certain tradesmen. Workers, coach-drivers... it was an everyday part of their vocabulary. It had little relevance (if any) to the number of ladies or gents in a given location. The sort of mechanical salutation you hear every day in hairdresser's, restaurants, cafés...

What a fool I had been! The words used by the coachman had no bearing whatsoever on whether Urbin was alone or accompanied by others. Urbin could just as easily have travelled home solo. *Have a good evening, ladies and gents!* And there might have been no ladies, and just a single gent.... This called everything into question.

That same evening I paid a visit to the stable where the coachman kept his horse, and where he himself slept. Getting inside was easy. Then I waited patiently for the man who looked like Paul Verlaine to return. As soon as I heard him coming, I hid.

I had brought with me a length of rope and an unloaded revolver. I would not need to use it. Shortly after he had stretched out on his cot, the coachmen fell asleep. He woke to find me standing over him.

"Whatever you do," I told him, "don't make a sound."

I brandished a pair of scissors and a straight razor close to his face. He thought I was about to cut his throat. He trembled.

In fact, it was only his beard I was interested in. I wanted to see that chin of his. For three months I had wondered about that man's chin. I needed to see it more desperately than the face of my mother, my father, or a certain beautiful girl... but enough about that. The chin was the thing. What sort of chin, I wondered, was lurking under that tangle of carrot-colored hair? It might be the proof I was looking for. It might be just what I needed to justify my theory.

It took less than ten minutes. The horse watched me with interest, but the coachman simply lay there in silent fury. He had no idea what I thought I was doing. Finally, I saw the chin. An almost non-existent, receded chin. If Urbin had a donkey's jaw, then this was a rat's.

So I was right!

A fact which had struck me about the description of Urbin's male companion was that he differed from the old bibliophile in almost every single way—apart from the chin. Operating under the assumption that the coachman was guilty, I had come up with the following theory: the coachman went into the house with Urbin. The two men were alone—Urbin had neither a man nor a woman with him that night. Very well. In order to pay the coachman, Urbin looked in a drawer for some loose change, for he only had banknotes with him. He paid his fare; on his way out, the coachman mechanically called out *Have a good evening, ladies and gents!*

A meaningless farewell, which finally made sense because it was meaningless. His mind was distracted as he headed out into the garden; haunted by the image of Urbin's well-stuffed wallet. At that moment he found the hammer lying on the ground...

The next day, he read my statement in the newspapers. He realized that I had been concealed in the house when he committed his crime. Perfect! This would enable him to provide descriptions of the non-existent "lady and gent" who had accompanied Urbin, and whose presence my testimony helped to confirm. He did not take too much effort with the woman: tall, slim, elegant, about thirty-two years old. Wearing brown... maybe. Blonde or brunette, he couldn't really tell. But the man— what sort of man should he conjure up? Simple, really. At that moment his brain was likely clouded with images of Urbin. But he knew that if he described Urbin, this would raise questions. So it was both logical and inevitable that he should describe this man as Urbin's exact physical opposite. While Urbin was short, this fellow was tall. Urbin wore a mustache, the other man was clean-shaven, and so forth...

But why had he not taken this parallel to its natural conclusion? Why give Urbin and his phantom killer identical chins?

Now I had the answer.

The coachman knew that if he gave Urbin's imaginary companion a grotesquely receded chin, he would in fact be describing
his own. Never mind the fact that he wore a long beard—he
wasn't willing to take the risk. He felt as though he would be
betraying himself. So he reversed the parallel, and gave the man
a chin that was the opposite of his own—and therefore identical to Urbin's!

The rest was simple. I told him I had witnessed what he'd
done. After a short while, the poor fellow confessed. He pointed
me in the direction of Urbin's wallet. I noticed seven thousand-
franc notes before I slipped it into my pocket, to say nothing of
the hundred-franc notes which I didn't trouble to count.

# POLICE TECHNIQUE

Not far from Fresnes Prison, the ironically named Avenue de la Liberté was full of kids, shouting and throwing stones into the oily water of the Bièvre.

Irritated, the policeman closed the window. He was heavy-set, and had a way of cocking his head which was reminiscent of a bull. He drummed on the window, then turned and walked towards a miserable-looking individual:

"You may as well confess. Your defense is absurd. You're the only one who could have done it; if you confess, you save your head. Don't be childish."

"For the last time, I'm innocent!"

The suspect had an emaciated face, with a high forehead made higher still by a rapidly receding hairline. His eyes were uneasy, hidden beneath a prominent brow.

A second policeman, sitting on the bed, shrugged, but said nothing.

"You're lying," the first resumed. "Why did you attack your cousin?"

"I didn't!"

The suspect's name was Marcel Lemoine. With a trembling hand he raised a cigarette to his lips. His face was a mass of tics. He had long, spindly fingers; his left thumb was stained with red. But it was not blood, it was vermilion. Lemoine was a painter. He was a weak man, but he had not yet cracked. The investigators, who were convinced of his guilt and believed him to be at the end of his tether, on the verge of confession, did not let up.

"Why did you do it? What was the motive?"

"I didn't!"

The policeman raised his arm in a frustrated motion, as though he were about to strike Lemoine, who recoiled, yelling: "You don't have the right!"

The policeman dropped his arm, spat into the fireplace and growled: "Vermin."

Marcel Lemoine ran for the door.

"Where are you going?"

"I've had enough! I'm innocent. I refuse to answer your questions any longer. First of all, I haven't been charged, have I? Not yet, anyway. So..."

"We won't keep you, pal, don't worry..."

"How dare you address me in that familiar tone!" yelled Lemoine. "I want out! Do you hear me? Let me out now!"

This was it. The young man had lost any semblance of composure, and was no longer even listening to the words that escaped his mouth.

"Lemoine?" the policeman seated on the bed called after him. Lemoine hesitated. "One more question, sir, if you don't mind?" (This policeman spoke in a more respectful tone.) "A simple question..." He lay back on the pillow and stared at the ceiling. "Suppose you are innocent. In that case, why won't you help us?"

"Because I don't know anything!"

"Let's see. Let's go through it again together. This morning, at eight o'clock, your father, M. Jean Lemoine, and your uncle, M. René Lemoine, leave the house on foot, heading for the Bourg-la-Reine station to catch the train to Paris. Ten minutes later M. Caffier, your cousin's fiancé, arrives by car. He talks to you for a few moments in your studio on the first floor, then spends about an hour on the ground floor with Mlle. At a quarter past nine, he leaves.

"Mlle Yvette sees him out and then returns to her room. From then on, you are alone in the house with your cousin. The two servants, Jean Noel and his wife Anna, are gardening out front of the house. Several neighbors have testified that Jean and Anna were out there non-stop until ten-thirty a.m., at which point Mme Anna Noel enters the house to prepare lunch and discovers Mlle Yvette lying on the floor of her room. Mme Anna Noel immediately alerts her husband; neighbors come running, a doctor finds that Mlle Yvette has received two violent blows to the right temporal region, administered with a blunt instrument which has not yet been found."

Marcel Lemoine grew impatient.

Downstairs, a doctor, Yvette Lemoine's two uncles, and Caffier, her fiancé, waited at the young woman's bedside. Yvette had not succumbed to her injuries, but she had been in a coma since the morning.

"What's the use of repeating the same story twenty times?"

Marcel Lemoine said upstairs. "You haven't asked me a question..."

"I'm getting there. All the windows overlooking the back and sides of the house were found locked from the inside. The Noel couple, who were out front, did not see anyone enter the house. A search revealed that no one was hiding anywhere inside. At a quarter past nine, Mlle Yvette was unharmed. At half past ten, she was found unconscious, at death's door. From a quarter past nine to ten-thirty, only two people were in the house: your cousin and you. If it wasn't you, then how did it happen? And who is responsible?"

"How should I know?" exclaimed Lemoine. "That's your job. I'm not a policeman; I'm an artist!"

He walked over to a canvas on a nearby easel; his latest work: an undergrowth—a nightmarish forest of dead trees, haunted by slimy creatures, and in the center of which gleamed a pool of dark water; an imaginative piece which was no doubt the product of a troubled mind.

"I was working on this painting. I heard nothing. I only learned what had happened when I heard the servant scream. I understand that everything points to me. But I'm innocent! Why should I want to hurt my cousin, when I care for her deeply? Even if I did have a motive, would I really be crazy enough to commit the crime when everyone knew I was alone in the house with Yvette?"

At that moment, the door opened, and a tall silhouette appeared in the doorway. It was Caffier, the fiancé, who worked for a large automotive firm.

"Quick!" he said. "Yvette's awake."

"Quick..."

This was also the word that the doctor murmured when the police entered. The girl had opened her eyes. The inspector began: "Can you hear me?"

He leaned in close. "Can you tell us who did this to you?"

The girl's eyelids fluttered; her lips moved; she was making a desperate effort to speak. The doctor and the inspector leaned in together and both heard these whispered words:

"My uncles..."

While the policeman asked everyone to leave the room, the doctor closed the dead woman's eyelids. Yvette Lemoine, a modern, lively young woman, with the short hair and firm features of

Diana the Huntress, whose face had the smoothness of marble, was already beginning to take on its coldness, too.

*

"So it was the uncles!" grumbled the bull-headed inspector a little later. "In that case, we need a motive. The whole thing's incredible."

He held out his hand to the artist: "I apologize.... Please forgive us...."

Lemoine burst into tears.

The case was indeed incredible, as the policeman had predicted, but not in the way he had predicted. Discovering the motive was easy enough—at least, one which would be admissible in court.

Eighteen-year-old Yvette Lemoine had been an orphan for four years. M. Jean Lemoine, father of the painter Marcel, and the young woman's uncle, was also her guardian. He was the trustee of the inheritance which would go to her when she came of age, or when she was married.

M. Jean Lemoine had been steadily losing money on the Stock Exchange. His brother René had sapped the rest. René was in the unfortunate profession of inventor; unfortunate because of the costs it entails. A bona fide genius, René Lemoine had shared his latest idea with his brother, who had generously advanced him a hefty sum. It was a marvelous invention: an ultra-light electronic capacitor capable of doubling the range of aircraft and making current planes obsolete overnight. An invention with limitless applications, which would no doubt be worth millions.

When M. Jean Lemoine's personal fortune dwindled, they had begun to cut into Yvette's inheritance. The prototypes were expensive, but they were getting closer and closer; success was imminent.

They proceeded in good faith. Two hundred thousand francs—a quarter of the young girl's fortune—had already been swallowed up, but the uncles would pay it all back. As soon as the invention began to yield a profit...

The only reason they had not discussed this "loan" with Yvette was it was simply that they did not wish to bother her with tedious money matters. There was no malice behind it.

Except, one fine day Yvette took a liking to Caffier, the automobile representative. This boy had neither the intelligence of M. René Lemoine nor the sensitivity of Marcel. But he played tennis like Borotra, swam like Taris, drove like Chiron, knew Paris—Paris la Nuit, in particular—better than any guide, and he had dazzling teeth, slick blond hair and handsome features.

Yvette met him in the corridors of the *police judiciaire*. He was there, he said pleasantly, "because there is just so much to learn." For her part, Yvette had gone to these esteemed premises for professional reasons: she was laboratory assistant to Professor Chapelain, the eminent forensic scientist.

From then on, the uncles had a motive: they had embezzled two-hundred thousand francs from Yvette; the wedding was a mere fortnight away; they were going to be found out.

Worse than that: they would have to abandon René Lemoine's invention. Caffier would not stand idly by while his wife's fortune was squandered on electronic capacitors.

The crime was less justifiable on a human level, as both men had real affection for their niece. But this was not enough to exonerate them. The passion for invention is no less likely than anything else— gambling, for instance— to lead to violence. And had Yvette not formally accused Jean and René Lemoine?

The difficulty lay in the fact that, on the day of the crime— indeed at the very hour when it took place—the two uncles were in Paris, in the office of the manager of a branch of the Société Générale, who, along with his assistant, was assessing their request for a short-term loan, with the possibility of obtaining a percentage of profits from René Lemoine's invention.

Jean and René Lemoine could not physically have committed the crime.

"Perhaps the poor girl was delirious?" the bull-headed policeman suggested.

The two uncles denied the accusation with all their might. They insisted that Yvette's last words had been misinterpreted. She had not spoken accusingly at all, but in affection, in farewell...

The police remained skeptical. Nevertheless, there was the indisputable alibi. The two uncles were released, but kept under surveillance.

It was then that Professor Chapelain resolved to take up the matter—partly because the mystery piqued his curiosity, and partly because of his affection for his deceased assistant. At the house on the avenue de la Liberté, he commenced a thorough investigation of the premises—without result. Next he returned to the Institute to examine the corpse.

Almost immediately, he spotted a gross oversight on the part of the police. Under Yvette Lemoine's nails, and threaded round her fingers, which nobody else had troubled to examine, he collected several hairs. Studying these hairs under a microscope enabled him to build up a description of the individual to whom they belonged: a young man, of robust constitution. Blond hairs interspersed with chestnut. Cut recently, they had undergone the following treatment: oil shampoo, lotion, brilliantine.

A comparison left no doubt about it: these hairs belonged to Caffier, Yvette's fiancé. Three days before the tragedy, Caffier had gone to his usual hairdresser. He'd had an oil shampoo, lotion rub, and he used brilliantine. A perfect match.

Professor Chapelain nodded to himself. He now understood where the police had gone wrong.

Caffier was the killer. After pretending to leave the house, he had in fact sneaked back inside. (How he managed to do that without being seen by the Noels or the neighbors remained to be seen, as did the motive.) Then he attacked his fiancée, without permitting her to catch a glimpse of his face. Perhaps he covered it with a handkerchief, or a scarf.... The first blow was insufficient. A struggle ensued, during which Yvette twisted a few of her attacker's hairs around her fingers, pulling them out of his scalp. And as she lay dying, she bravely remembered what she had learned in the laboratory, and used that knowledge to identify her killer with the hairs wrapped around her knuckles. "My knuckles..." was what she had said. But the men at her bedside misheard it as: "My uncles..."

Caffier provided an alibi. Upon leaving the house, he drove to Arpajon to visit a client. This was acknowledged as the truth. But Caffier had got to Arpajon late enough for anyone to suspect that he had not gone there directly. This is how he explained it: not far from Bourg-la-Reine, his car had broken down for half an hour or so in open country. Unfortunately for Caffier, two workmen claimed to have been working in the vicinity, picking up litter along the roadside. They would certainly have noticed the broken-down automobile—but they hadn't. Caffier had lied.

When questioned, he was forced to admit it. However, he refused to explain how he had really spent that missing thirty-five minutes.

"With a lady."

Though the officers pledged to exercise discretion, he refused to speak further. Moreover, like Marcel, Jean, and René Lemoine, he vehemently denied committing the crime or participating in it in any way.

Once he was officially under arrest, he was quick to hire the lawyer Prosper Lepicq to work on his defense.

"Isn't there something else you could try, Professor? There is a mystery here; a mystery that a scientist such as you must be able to elucidate. I'm absolutely convinced that my client is innocent. He has said things to me... in confidence. The explanation he gave me for this missing thirty-five minutes..."

"You mean the 'other woman'?"

"Yes. That explanation is false."

"Of course it is! The broken-down car was false, and now the affair is false. Caffier is hardly the most reliable fellow. But I'm afraid there's nothing more I can do. The hair is his. There's not much more to say."

For a minute, Prosper Lepicq stared at the professor with his murky eyes. Then he tried again. "Professor, Caffier's confidences, which I am not authorized to reveal, are of such a nature that they justify his silence regarding the use of his time. If he does not speak, he may be found guilty and guillotined. This is by no means a certainty. On the other hand, if he speaks, he *will* go to prison. He knows it. When in doubt, he prefers to remain silent."

"The hairs are Caffier's," the professor repeated dryly.

"May I ask you one more question?"

"Of course."

"How do you explain the fact that all the hairs found between Mlle Lemoine's fingers were cut, as though by a hairdresser, rather than wrenched from the scalp?"

"The explanation is simple enough. Yvette *did* wrench out several hairs as well as the shorter cuttings. But while the shorter hairs were more easily trapped between her knuckles, the same cannot be said of the longer hairs. They likely came loose from her hand while she was being carried to her bed, or during the eight hours in which she was in a coma. As such, it indicates gross negligence on the part of the police."

"Thank you, Professor. One last question. Would you be so kind as to part with one of these hairs for a day? I have a certain curiosity that I wish to satisfy."

"Indeed. There are in fact four hairs retrieved from the dead woman's hand."

"I'll take two, if you don't mind..."

Twenty-four hours later, Professor Chapelain received Prosper Lepicq's business card in an envelope with his compliments. On a sheet of paper, the two hairs had been carefully secured with narrow strips of tape.

\*

That same evening, two figures conversed face to face across a table. Or, more accurately, one of them—a tall, thin, youthful-looking fellow—was doing the talking. It was the lawyer, Prosper Lepicq. The other man listened with an attentive frown.

"You see, my friend, that the rule is the same for crime as it is for everything else: moderation is the key. Subtle, but not *too* subtle. If Chapelain had been in less of a hurry to close the case, he would have discovered the truth. I, however, did not fall into the same trap."

"What trap? I don't understand where you're coming from."

The evening was drawing in. The last rays of sunlight streamed through the windows.

"Be serious," said Lepicq. "I didn't come here as an enemy. You must understand. I am not a policeman; I'm a lawyer. It's only because there is an innocent man behind bars that I have come to find you. You, the murderer."

The man jumped.

"Me? Are you crazy? I'll..."

"You will be quiet and listen to me. Calmly. With your hands on the table. Please. Now! That's better.... Now we are going to study a problem of police technique.

"The murder charge is based on four fragments of hair found in the victim's hand. Chapelain has examined them, and established that they belong to Caffier. So Caffier is arrested. Now, I say that Chapelain was a little hasty. He neglected to consider the *age* of the hair. In other words, how *old* the hair was. Or, to put it plainly: *how long ago the hair had been cut*. I, however, *did* consider this. A forensic expert I asked to consider this question discovered that the hairs had been cut roughly ten days before the crime was committed. Therefore, the clippings found in Yvette Lemoine's hand could not have been from Caffier's trip to the hairdresser three days earlier. Before that, he had not been the hairdresser in some three weeks. Therefore, these hairs were not cut by the hairdresser at all."

Lepicq had taken a set square from the desk and was swinging it to punctuate his sentences.

"If not the hairdresser, then who? And why did these clippings remain in Caffier's hair? And how is it that during the struggle Mlle Lemoine's fingers only managed to collect clippings which had been taken ten days earlier?"

Suddenly, Lepicq leaned over and brought the set square down heavily on the fingers of the man sitting opposite him. There was a cry, and a heavy thump.

A revolver fell from the man's hand, and the lawyer sent it skidding to the corner of the room with a quick kick.

"I was watching you, my friend. Stay perfectly still, and I'll continue."

The man leaned on the table and buried his face in his hands.

The paintings adorning the walls and easels seemed to shift and change; their lurid colors and strange, fantastical scenes moved in and out of focus.

"Marcel Lemoine, *you* murdered your cousin. You had formed your audacious plan long before you put it into action. You deliberately chose the most 'dangerous' moment: the time when you would be completely alone with your cousin. In a way, this was a perfect alibi, as it would make your guilt seem all the more unlikely. But this was not your only precaution: you also had the hair clippings, which you yourself took from Caffier's head while he slept in the house one night.

"The day of the crime, you entered your cousin's room without attracting her attention. You struck her before she could get a look at you. She dropped to the floor. You thought she was dead. So you placed the hair clippings between her fingers.

"But Yvette was only stunned. And in her half-conscious state she felt you doing something to her fingers and her knuckles. (It's not so easy, is it, to place hair clippings in an inanimate hand?) Yvette moved a little; perhaps she gave a moan. You struck her a second time.

"How delighted you must have been when Chapelain discovered those clippings! Had he not done so, you would have arranged for them to be discovered yourself. It was not enough that your cousin should die. Above all, you wanted Caffier to be convicted of the crime.

"Because you really did love your cousin. You loved her more than anything in the world; more than your art itself. No doubt you had confessed your love to her. I imagine her letting you down gently, softly pushing you away. That must have been very painful. But you remained her close friend and confidant, and consigned your unrequited love to the status of a daydream. In appearance, at least. In fact, you had never hated anything in this world quite as much as you hated Caffier, this ordinary young man who had none of your sensitivity or spirit, but who was nonetheless handsome, full of life, and a devil with the ladies..."

With his head still buried in his hands, Marcel Lemoine did not reply.

"Tortured by your inferiority complex, painting those disturbing, angry paintings, growing ever more obsessed, you kept a close eye on your love rival. How delighted you must have been when you discovered that this pretty boy was in fact a petty thief—a mere conscript in a vast criminal enterprise. Did you tell Yvette? And did she answer that she didn't care, that she would marry Caffier anyway, and convince him to abandon his life of crime? I do not know.

"In any case, you discovered that Caffier was meeting with his accomplices between nine-fifteen am and ten am. Your father and your uncle were going to Paris that same morning. You decided that today was the day. You committed your crime. And then, the following day, you telephoned Caffier and impersonated one of the members of his band of thieves. You said something along the lines of: 'Tell the police whatever you have to, but if you mention us then your life won't be worth living.' And so you guaranteed not only Caffier's silence—but also his guilt in the eyes of the law.

Lepicq stood up.

"Come now, Lemoine, be a man! It's not too late. You still have a chance to make things right. You are going to turn yourself in, and I will defend you. I will save you from the guillotine. Your inferiority complex, your tortured artist's soul, your sexual repression, your unrequited love... I'll have the jury in the palm of my hand! You'll be out in five years, do you hear me?"

Lepicq placed his hand on the artist's shoulder.

"Five years, Lemoine. Five. No more."

He gripped the artist's shoulder and shook it. The chair wobbled, spilling Marcel Lemoine onto the floor. He was dead.

On his right hand, Lepicq found a ring with an empty bezel. Lemoine had poisoned himself.

"The fool!" the lawyer growled. "Insanity... it was a ready-made plea."

# THE DISAPPEARANCE OF EMMELINE POKE

## 1. STATEMENT OF THE KING OF PRUSSIA

Before his interview with M. de Saint-Ignace (the *juge d'instruction* who had arrived from Barbezieux that morning), the King of Prussia extinguished his cigarette between two fingernails. Then he slipped it behind his ear and pushed open the door. He disappeared inside, leaving Charente's Grande Place de Châteaurenard occupied by only four old men gossiping on a bench, and a gang of kids who were infinitely more concerned with the capabilities of a bike derailleur on display in the window of M. Cocagne's shop than they were with the mysterious "Poke affair."

M. Coulemelle, the justice of the peace, had placed his office at the disposal of the *juge d'instruction*. He himself was seated at the back of the room, almost invisible in a shadowed corner.

"Monsieur Fenetrange, isn't it? Guillaume Fenetrange?"

"Correct, sir. Though I am also known in these parts as the 'King of Prussia.' That's on account of my first name, and also because I speak a little German."

M. de Saint-Ignace's throat swelled, as though with a goitre. Along with his bulbous eyes, this made him look like a frog. It was a reflex brought on by surprise or irritation, which was all the more unfortunate because he was otherwise rather good-looking.

The King of Prussia was a little embarrassed, and fidgeted in his chair as he added, absurdly: "I also speak a little English." Then he laughed. "I'm sorry, *monsieur le juge*. You didn't ask me here to find out if I speak English or German.... I might as well tell you that I'm a hard worker and a decent typist! I sound as though I'm looking for a job..."

The *juge d'instruction* deigned to smile, his throat resumed its usual shape, and M. de Saint-Ignace—once again the handsome lad who had broken the heart of more than one young lady over in Barbezieux—studied the King of Prussia with interest.

The man had the appearance of a gentle giant. Over six feet
in height; blond, curly hair; blue eyes. He was dressed in white
linen, wore espadrilles, and a large imitation Panama hat. Defi-
nitely out of place among these men in suits.

"It's about the Poke affair, M. Fenetrange. I brought you here
to hear your statement concerning the events you witnessed
in *Prends-Tu-Garde* wood at nine o'clock last Sunday morning.
That is to say, the unexplained disappearance of Mlle Emmeline Poke. I would also like to make it clear that I don't take
you for an ordinary witness. I understand that you're something
of an intellectual."

"I merely grow flowers, sir, and sell them," said the King of
Prussia, evidently flattered. "But aside from horticulture, I don't
deny that I have written my share of letters to *La Petite Gironde*
and *La Liberté du Sud-Ouest*..."

The stenographer began to take notes: "Friday July 13, 1934.
Statement of Fenetrange, Guillaume, a.k.a. the King of Prussia,
horticulturist and man of letters, residing at l'impasse des Cou-
drettes in Châteaurenard..."

"Very well. Last Sunday," declared the King of Prussia, "I was
in *Prends-Tu-Garde* wood. I had gone there to research a pet proj-
ect of mine. I am very interested in magic both black and white,
and it is my dream to write an academic paper on the occult."

M. de Saint-Ignace made an impatient gesture.

"The weather was very clear, and it was bright even in the
midst of the wood. It was already warm, and the air was still
and clear. I distinctly heard the town hall clock strike nine. My
hearing is excellent. I was sitting near a path lined with walnut
trees when I saw a man and a woman out for a stroll. I recognized Ange Poke, and got the impression that the woman was
his sister Emmeline. Ange was smoking a cigarette."

"How far away were you?"

"Very close, *monsieur le juge*. Less than two feet away."

"Then why do you say you *recognized* Ange Poke, but merely
*got the impression* that the woman was his sister Emmeline?"

"Merely being scrupulous, *monsieur le juge*. I recognized Ange
by his voice. He said to me: 'Morning, King of Prussia.' I replied,
'Morning, Ange.' He joked: 'I'm just walking Emmeline home,
in case she gets lost.' The two brothers, Ange and Jules Poke,
live on the edge of *Prends-Tu-Garde* wood, in an isolated shack.
A few miles away, on the other side of the wood, their sister lives

in an equally isolated little place. The woods are not particularly dense, so I thought it unlikely Emmeline would get lost! I spoke to her, too, but she didn't answer. Instead she just started sneezing. 'Ah, you have hay fever, Emmeline!' I said. "'Yes,' said Ange, 'it's hay fever. It's a real nuisance!' That's why I cannot say that I *recognized* Emmeline that morning, because she did not speak to me. But of course, it must have been her."

"Forgive me, but I'm still not sure I understand...."

"I am long-sighted. *Very* long-sighted. Of course you will say to me: 'Wear spectacles!' But do you know how much they cost? A hundred francs per lens. I used to own a pair, but one day I dropped them and stepped on them by accident. So, I decided to make do without. I can see very well from a distance, but unfortunately Emmeline was just a bit too close....

"And you mustn't forget that she was also wearing a *quichenotte*. That's a local word, sir. You know, those headdresses that shield the face and quite a bit of the neck. I understand that the word *quichenotte* is a distortion of the English: 'Kiss not.' It entered popular usage around the time that the English occupied Saintonge, which was ceded to them by King Louis...."

"Please go on," said the judge impatiently, indifferent to this etymological detail.

"So, the two Pokes passed me by. I got up and set off on a walk parallel to their route. Intermittently, I glimpsed their silhouettes moving behind the curtain of foliage. On the edge of the wood, brother and sister parted ways; Emmeline headed through the field on the way to her house, while Ange headed back the way he had come. He was returning home. Ten seconds later, I also reached the edge of the wood.

"Then, a strange feeling struck me. A kind of... absence, you know? I didn't understand it until I recognized Emmeline's roof in the distance.

"What was 'absent' from the landscape was Emmeline. Agility not being her strong point—she is in her fifties, I believe—she couldn't have gone far, and yet I didn't see her. I assumed she had perhaps lain down somewhere in the shade and thought no more of it. That's all, *monsieur le juge*. Subsequently, when I learned that I had been the last to see the poor woman, I was utterly dumbfounded!"

M. de Sainte-Ignace, who had leaned forward to hear better,

sat back to meditate on this. Finally, he straightened up. "Monsieur Fenetrange, thank you. I won't detain you any longer."

The King of Prussia quickly crossed the Grande Place, for the sun was beating down. He gave a melancholy thought to his flowers, which were beginning to wilt in spite of frequent waterings. Then he began to sing softly, to a tune of his own, in French, English and German, these words: "*Chérie, je t'aime,* Darling, I love you, *Mein schatz, ich liebe dich...*"

This was in fact the only sentence the gentle giant could say in either English or German. And Guillaume Fenetrange had no particular desire to learn any more, utterly convinced that this phrase was all an intelligent man needed in order to get by in a foreign land.

This "King of Prussia" was somewhat naïve, you might say.

## 2. THE STATEMENT OF MAX PAPILLON

"What do you make of it, Coulemelle?" asked the *juge d'instruction.*

The justice of the peace opened his mouth but said nothing. For four days, he had meditated on this strange disappearance without managing to form an opinion.

"Let's take it from the beginning," said M. de Saint-Ignace. "A fifty-eight-year-old lady visits her day-laborer brothers, who are aged forty-three and forty-seven respectively. One of her brothers escorts her through the wood again on her way home. They part ways scarcely a hundred meters from her house. But she never gets home. Nobody sees her again, or finds any trace of her. She is vanished in broad daylight, a stone's throw from Châteaurenard. The brothers know absolutely nothing. *We* know... nothing." He mimed blowing a speck of dust from his palm. "On the edge of the wood, a short stretch of countryside, and Emmeline Poke is gone. Not even so much as a single hair remains. The two houses are searched from top to bottom, the wood has been excavated thoroughly, every square inch of land explored, the lakes dragged, the wells... there is no river nearby, nor quarry....

"Police from outside the area are alerted, the search is widened to include all the train and bus services in the region. The story is circulated in the press. All in vain. She is gone—like magic, as the King of Prussia would say."

"I don't believe in magic," said the justice of the peace.

"Me neither. Therefore, we must study the problem rationally in order to perceive the rational solution. Firstly, I note that at nine o'clock on the Sunday morning in question, M. Fenetrange was not alone in *Prends-Tu-Garde* wood with Ange and Emmeline Poke. Also present was one Max Papillon, a farmhand and sometime poacher—a man of questionable character. I have had him brought in."

At that moment, there came a knock on the door. A round-faced sergeant, whose skin was the color of a ripe tomato, appeared. "Papillon is here, monsieur le juge."

"Bring him in."

The sergeant ushered in a fellow of about forty, who was medium height, with an enormous head and spindly legs. He also sported an unruly beard and mop of hair. On hearing that they simply wanted to question him about what he saw five days earlier in *Prends-Tu-Garde* wood, he breathed a sigh of relief.

The stenographer had already begun to make notes: *Statement of Papillon, Max, farmhand residing with his employer, M. Pillegrain, in route de Chalais, Châteaurenard. Date: Friday 13th...*

The sergeant sat discreetly beside M. Coulemelle.

"To be honest," Max Papillon said sharply, "I don't know a thing."

"No need to speak so loud," said the *juge d'instruction*. "I'm not deaf." He then asked: "Did you see Emmeline Poke and her brother Ange that morning?"

"As I see you, Judge."

"How far away were you?"

"Quite far. Some fifty meters or so. But I can see well enough."

"Did you recognize them?"

"I recognized Ange, sir. Emmeline was a different story. She was wearing a *quichenotte*. But of course it was her, who else could it have been? I called out to them, I said 'Ah, young lovers!' as a sort of joke, you know. They both gestured in my direction, which I took to be their answer."

"Both of them?"

"Certainly, sir," Papillon said, surprised.

M. de Saint-Ignace heaved a sigh of satisfaction. "So you recognized Emmeline Poke by her voice..."

Papillon laughed. "Ah! No, sir. No!"

"What do you mean?"

"I'm hard of hearing, *monsieur le juge*. From that distance, I couldn't make out a word."

"This is absurd," grumbled M. de Saint-Ignace, "we're getting nowhere."

He resumed his questioning: "Did you see Ange Poke alone afterward?"

"Yes, monsieur le juge. About five minutes later. I was lying behind a tuft of beggar's buttons."

"Pardon?"

"It's a plant. That's what we call it round here, anyway."

"He means burdock," said M. Coulemelle.

"So," resumed the farm-hand, "I was lying behind those beggar's buttons when I saw Ange pass by. He was walking all right. And that's all there was to it."

"Did you meet M. Fenetrange in the wood?"

"The King of Prussia? No, *monsieur le juge*."

"What were you doing in *Prends-Tu-Garde* wood that morning?"

"It was Sunday, sir. I was relaxing. Some go to church. Me, I prefer to lie down in the shade. You've got to find peace wherever you can."

"Thank you, M. Papillon."

Now, the *juge d'instruction* was considerably more cheerful. "This is a very carefully orchestrated affair," he said. "But the question remains, is it kidnapping or murder? I am leaning towards murder. I doubt we shall see Emmeline Poke alive again."

"Aren't you jumping the gun a little, my friend?" M. Coulemelle protested. "Why couldn't Emmeline have disappeared of her own volition?"

M. de Saint-Ignace shook his head impetuously. "A woman of her age? How would she have pulled it off? She didn't fly away in a balloon, did she?"

"But in that case, who's responsible? Ange Poke? Papillon? Fenetrange?"

M. de Saint-Ignace adopted his most Mephistophelean smile. "There were four people in *Prends-Tu-Garde* wood that morning. Ange and Emmeline Poke, Papillon and Fenetrange. Neither Ange Poke, nor Max Papillon, nor Guillaume Fenetrange murdered Emmeline Poke. And yet, Emmeline Poke was murdered."

The justice of the peace, the sergeant, and the stenographer were all observing him carefully.

"Come now, my friend, surely you must..."

"No, my dear Coulemelle. You must *not*. This whole thing is both extremely clever and remarkably childish. Listen: Ange Poke and his sister Emmeline head out through the wood. The first witness they encounter is Max Papillon. Papillon has good eyesight, but he is hard of hearing. Therefore he is unable to converse with Emmeline. Both the brother and the sister speak to him, but because of the distance and his deafness, he does not hear them. The second witness they encounter is Guillaume Fenetrange. Fenetrange is sitting on the edge of the path, but he is extremely long-sighted. Emmeline passes too close for him to distinguish her clearly. However, Fenetrange has perfect hearing. Therefore, if Emmeline speaks... but she does not speak. Instead, she sneezes. Hay fever, her brother explains.

"This leads us to the inevitable conclusion: that woman was not Emmeline Poke. But Ange sought to pass her off as Emmeline. I suppose that before he escorted her through the wood, he took a look around and saw Papillon and Fenetrange. This was a stroke of good luck. He knew he could take advantage of the first man's deafness and the other's long-sightedness. What perfect witnesses they would make, to confirm that Emmeline Poke must have been alive on July the eighth! This false Emmeline simply had to pass by at a good distance from the deaf man and to ensure she did not speak as she passed by the long-sighted one!"

"But this is fantastic! Who could this false Emmeline be? And why would Ange Poke...? And besides, we still have not solved the mystery of her disappearance at the edge of the wood...."

"But there is no mystery! You see, my dear Coulemelle, this false Emmeline was not a woman at all, but *Jules Poke dressed in his sister's clothes.* At the edge of the wood, what did he do? Why, he simply removes the dress and the *quichenotte.* Of course it goes without saying that he is wearing his everyday clothes underneath. He throws himself flat on his stomach and, with the dress and the quichenotte under his arm, he crawls back to the shack where his brother Ange is now waiting for him. And so Emmeline Poke has vanished!

"And the reason for this performance? The Poke brothers murdered their sister, either on the morning of the eighth or the day before. Perhaps even two or three days before. If that were the case, Jules could simply have taken her place. After all, she hardly went out, except into Châteaurenard on market days. She hardly ever received visitors. Her brothers brought most of her supplies. The only danger was the baker's cart, which came by twice a week...."

"So the Poke brothers wanted to make it seem as though Emmeline was alive when she was dead?"

"You've got it."

"With what motive?"

"Hopefully further investigation will bring this to light. Did Emmeline Poke have money?"

"Not to my knowledge. What about you, sergeant?"

"Nor mine sir," the sergeant answered.

On his return home that day, the sergeant scrupulously reported these events to his wife, before concluding: "He's a clever fellow, that judge. And those brothers are a pair of fiends!"

"Oh be quiet," said his wife. "They might be innocent, you know."

"Oh really? Then whom do you suspect? Me, maybe?"

"Idiot."

"In any case, if M. de Saint-Ignace is right then he'll be heading straight for a promotion. Maybe they'll give him the top job in Angoulême?"

"Why not?" said the lady. "After all, he's handsome enough."

That same day, Ange and Jules Poke were arrested and charged with the murder of their sister. They denied it—Jules with dignity, Ange with considerable fury.

## 3. RADIESTHESIA

Excavations undertaken in the immediate vicinity of the brothers' shack did not yield a corpse. Though the murderers were in custody, the mystery of Emmeline Poke's disappearance remained.

The authorities were no closer to resolving this question when, ten days after the arrests, Guillaume Fenetrange presented himself once again at the office of M. de Saint-Ignace and requested a confidential meeting.

"Here, *monsieur le juge...*"

The King of Prussia had taken from his pocket an old leather purse and a pendulum: a small metal ball attached to a strand of thread.

"I have already told you, *monsieur le juge*, that I am interested in the occult and, more generally speaking, phenomena which remains unexplained by science. Dowsing has nothing to do with magic. And yet it fascinates me. I had the idea of trying to influence the pendulum with the aid of this leather money purse, which was given to me by Emmeline Poke. Then I held the pendulum above a map of the area and observed its oscillations. Can you guess where it led me?"

"I've no idea," said a skeptical and indifferent M. de Saint-Ignace.

"The Châteaurenard cemetery," said the King of Prussia gravely.

The judge jumped. The cemetery? No one had thought of looking for Emmeline Poke's body in the cemetery.

"Please go on."

"To find out for sure, I went to the cemetery. I let myself be guided by my pendulum. Above a particular grave, it gave the same number of oscillations as above the purse. It was a fresh grave, *monsieur le juge.*"

"A fresh grave? Whose?"

"For the name to mean anything to you, you must first know that about six months ago, a woman from Cognac came to settle in Châteaurenard, in a place on rue Haute, on the edge of town. A seventy-five-year-old woman named Elisa Deschamps. As anyone will tell you, it was generally believed that she was sitting on a very nice nest egg. And yet she lived alone, no servants. Two and a half months ago, Mlle Deschamps suffered a stroke which left her paralyzed. She could still speak and move her arms, but her legs were finished. Nevertheless, she still refused to engage a servant. For a few francs a month, one of her neighbors would prepare a meal for her and leave it at her bedside, and sometimes help out around the house as the need arose."

"What are you getting at?"

"This, *monsieur le juge*. The Deschamps woman was found dead in her bed of another stroke on the morning of July eighth."

"And?"

"July eighth is the day Emmeline Poke disappeared."

"I don't follow."

"According to the doctor, Deschamps must have died on the evening of July seventh. Now mark this, *monsieur le juge.* Elisa Deschamps had no family, and she was to be buried in the Châteaurenard cemetery. The gravedigger, Amédée, is not a man to waste time, on account of the fact that he's also a mason and a farmer. So he had finished digging her grave by sundown on July eighth, even though the priest has only just decided that the burial would take place on the morning of the ninth. And my pendulum, under the influence of Emmeline Poke's purse, led me right to Elisa Deschamps's grave!"

"What? So you're saying..."

"There may be nothing to it, *monsieur le juge*. But I couldn't help but wonder if that open grave had proved a convenient hiding place for a second corpse. All they had to do was dig a little deeper during the night of the eighth, drop Emmeline in and then pack the soil on top! Emmeline wasn't a big woman; there was little risk of leaving excess soil."

Two days later, the excavation took place. The grave of Elisa Descamps was opened and her coffin removed. They dug. And, about a foot below the coffin, they unearthed the body of Emmeline Poke. She had been strangled.

The following day, the King of Prussia was all over the papers. He had never been so popular, and the demand for his work was at an all-time high from all corners of France.

All the same, M. de Saint-Ignace remained uneasy. He was in desperate need of some piece of evidence which might compel the Poke brothers to confess. Because they continued to deny any part in the crime.

Then, after a lengthy period of contemplation, the *juge d'instruction* had an idea. He immediately headed back to Châteaurenard, to pay a visit to the King of Prussia. He was in need of his services once again.

"Monsieur Fenetrange... That leather purse which Emmeline Poke gave you, how long have you had it?"

"Oh, a long time, *monsieur le juge*. A year and a half. Maybe two."

"Really? And yet, after all that time, it still influenced the pendulum. Do you think it could work with a photograph as well?"

"A photograph of the murderers?"

"Well," the *juge* equivocated, "let's just call them suspects."

"I couldn't say for sure," replied Fenetrange, "but it can't hurt to try."

M. de Saint-Ignace drew two photographs from his pocket.

"In my opinion, these are the two men who killed Emmeline Poke."

The King of Prussia went pale and looked at the *juge d'instruction* in bewilderment. One of the photographs showed himself, and the other showed Max Papillon.

"The purse which you claim Emmeline Poke gifted to you a year and a half ago, perhaps two, was in fact the property of Elisa Deschamps, who had been living in Châteaurenard a mere six months."

Guillaume Fenetrange told the whole story immediately. Emmeline Poke spent a great deal of money on herself. Max Papillon spent money on women. Guillaume Fenetrange spent money on his occult research.

Together, the three of them plotted to steal from Elisa Deschamps. While Emmeline sat at her bedside, Papillon and Fenetrange—both masked—searched the adjoining rooms for the old woman's loot. They did not find it. But Papillon made a great deal of noise when trying to force the locked drawer of a sideboard. This startled Fenetrange, who knocked over a chair. Emmeline Poke tried to explain it away to Mlle Deschamps: "It's a rat," she had said. But the invalid had fixed her with a strange look. Then, the old woman who had been bedbound for over two months, suddenly sat up, stretching out her arm towards the open door. Papillon and Fenetrange, fearing discovery, had fled into the corridor. They hadn't yet removed the colored scarves which shielded their features and they had no idea that a mirrored wardrobe in Elisa Deschamps's room had reflected their disquieting images. A few seconds later, the old lady fell back on her pillows, dead of fright.

What to do?

Get out of there as soon as possible? Emmeline would have none of it. They had come so far, she reasoned, that a mere death could not stand between them and their loot. So she searched.

Throughout July the seventh, Emmeline played the part of the invalid whenever neighbors came calling, bidding them to stay away. Then she got up and continued her search for the elusive nest egg.

The next day, Sunday, when the neighbors discovered Elisa Deschamps dead in her bed, Papillon and Fenetrange waited for Emmeline Poke in *Prends-Tu-Garde* wood.

Ange Poke walked her to the edge of the wood, and as soon

as he left, the men approached her. Had she found anything? No, she said. In fact, she had left the house in rue Haute empty-handed. But Papillon perceived something in her expression... He grabbed her, searched her and found sewn into her petticoat a leather purse containing sixty thousand francs in large notes.

Emmeline struggled, screamed.... Papillon's fingers twined around her throat. And so he became a murderer.

The idea of hiding the body in Elisa Deschamps' grave came from Papillon, too. But the business of the false statements, where the two men played discreetly on their deafness and long-sightedness respectively, came from Fenetrange.

The plan was to make the authorities suspect that the woman they saw in *Prends-Tu-Garde* wood was not really Emmeline. From then on, the brothers would inevitably fall under suspicion. In addition, by "discovering" the corpse thanks to his dowsing, the King of Prussia intended to place himself above suspicion and to gain publicity for his research. But he made one mistake: he incorrectly assumed the leather purse belonged to Emmeline Poke. He had reckoned without her greed and laziness. For not only had she made up her mind to keep the sixty thousand francs to herself, but could not even bring herself to get rid of a worn-out old purse.

In the back of the van which was carrying him to the prison in Barbezieux, Guillaume Fenetrange was singing softly to himself: "Darling, I love you... *Mein schatz, ich liebe dich...*"

"What are you talking about?" growled Max Papillon, who was sitting beside him. "Speak up. You know very well that I can't hear!"

The King of Prussia shrugged. Even if he had sung at the top of his lungs, Max Papillon would not have understood. Max Papillon, who spoke no foreign languages...

Ten months later, Fenetrange and Papillon were sentenced to eight years' hard labor. By then, the "handsome" M. de Saint-Ignace (to borrow a phrase from the sergeant's wife) had already been rewarded for his perspicacity—with the "top job" over in Angoulême.

# THE TALE OF
# A TARTLET

## 1. PIPO, THE MAN FROM THE ELECTRIC COMPANY

Léon Petitquartier was waiting. He was no longer thinking; he'd given up trying to think. He wore an expression of ecstasy. In fact, he was utterly stupefied. His lips moved, but he didn't say a word. In his mind he was watching an endless cinema reel, rolling backwards and forwards. A succession of simple images, with one detail always the same—three letters printed on a label (CNK)—transformed it from an ordinary, innocuous picture into a tragedy. A tragedy that only Léon Petitquartier could comprehend.

Leaning against the pewter bar, nursing a coffee, Léon waited for the announcement of the inevitable event; the event which had perhaps already taken place; the event that would make him a murderer. In the large barroom of the café on place Biancour, four men were chatting loudly amongst themselves. They were: an insurance clerk, a postman, a bank clerk, and a cashier from the electric company. They were getting ready for a game of darts—it was a harmless tradition they indulged in every Sunday. Leaning against the billiard table, the landlord (who wouldn't be joining in with the game) had his gaze fixed on the dartboard as well.

The postman, a fellow whose clogged arteries would likely condemn him to an early death, carefully placed one foot flush with a chalk line on the floor, raised the dart to eye level, and aimed. His throwing arm grew tense. A fellow in corduroys had just appeared in the doorway, dragging a bicycle by the handlebars.

"Watch the billiard balls, Ernest," the landlady yelped at her husband. "Here comes Houdini!"

The new arrival headed straight for the cashier from the electric company. "Hey, Cigogne, have you heard the latest?"

"Quiet, let the man throw," Cigogne replied distractedly, his gaze fixed on the dart board with a level of intensity to match that of the man who was actually throwing the dart.

But the new arrival would not be deterred. "It's Pipo. You know Pipo? Well, Pipo's finished. Dead. Bought the farm. Cashed his chips in. Near l'Étang de la Ville, that's where they found him. I was there, I saw it for myself. I was pedaling this beast for dear life-" (he shook the bicycle vigorously, bouncing it on its tires) "—I saw the whole thing. The Italian was in a dreadful state when they found him. Looked as if he'd had a dose of rat poison."

A loud clatter: with a clumsy gesture, Léon Petitquartier had just spilled his drink. He grimaced, smiled apologetically, and for a moment or two seemed absorbed in contemplation of the liquid which now flooded the pewter bar. Then he explained: "So sorry. I'm not feeling too good this morning."

At the same moment, the postman asked the newcomer: "What are you babbling about, Houdini?"

The other man did not answer right away. He did his best to wedge the bicycle upright and addressed Léon: "What's the matter with you? Got up on the wrong side of bed this morning?"

"Must have done," said Léon with an embarrassed chuckle.

"Well," the other man resumed, "I was saying that less than half an hour ago they found the Italian, Pipo, dead. Feet in the manure, face down in a heap of broken bottles and sardine cans, a stone's throw from l'Étang de la Ville. Pipo worked at your place, l'Ouest-Lumière, right, Cigogne?"

"Yes. He was a laborer. How did he die?"

Although Léon Petitquartier had been expecting this to happen—in fact, he could hardly have expected anything else—the news still came as a shock. He felt empty, devoid of feeling. Utterly numb. And that interminable film in his head had frozen on its final tableau: a man stretched out among broken bottles and empty sardine cans, his feet buried in a pile of manure. And, in the corner of the screen, a discreet signature comprised only initials, three trembling letters: CNK

Well, there it was. Poisoned. Léon Petitquartier, aged seventeen, son of M. Paul Petitquartier (collector of arachnids) and Mme. Anna Petitquartier (pastry chef), who lived with his parents in rue Ludovic-Petau-de-Maulette, in Montfort-l'Amaury (Seine-et-Oise); Léon Petitquartier, who was studying a correspondence course in accounting with the École Pigier in Paris, was now a murderer. In a kind of haze, the adolescent could no longer speak or even taste the coffee on his tongue. All he could do was think: *Pipo... only an Italian, after all... it could have been worse...*

He forced himself to smile. And then his ears pricked up.

"An embolism, so the police are saying," continued the man with the bicycle, the man they called "Houdini."

Léon downed what was left of his coffee, then said to the landlord: "Check, please."

A moment later, this shrewd young man was on the move.

"Care to join us in a game?" Cigogne suggested.

"Just let me put my bike away," answered Houdini. "Back in a moment." Nimbly straddling the bicycle, the velvet-clad magician freewheeled out onto the rue de Paris.

"Embolism," murmured Léon Petitquartier bitterly, walking slowly across place Biancour toward rue Ludovic-Petau-de-Maulette. "Embolism! The fools..."

*

A pair of buses rolled imperiously into the square from the rue Amaury. They halted side by side in the dead center of the square, near the church gate, flanking a luxury, ocean-blue Mercedes which looked to have been abandoned. Travelers who had arrived at the station by the 8.26 am train dismounted: a dozen tourists, two landscape painters, two salesmen from Paris, and four old women with shopping bags who'd come from Plaisir-Grignon. It was 8.45.

Stumbling on the uneven cobblestones of rue Ludovic-Petau-de-Maulette, Léon headed back toward his mother's pâtisserie.

Tall and blond, with a handful of downy hairs sprouting from his chin, he was a bundle of loosely-bound bones on stilts. He walked like a marionette, or an automaton that might collapse at any moment. This was because of his eyesight, which was very poor indeed. He often felt as though he were traveling through fog, or as though the world around him was a confused blur which only resolved itself into shapes about ten meters away from him, at which point everything became sharply clear.

That morning, Léon was more unsteady than ever. His starched collar, minus tie, accentuated the burlesque nature of his appearance. His wallet was open in his left hand, while his right clutched a few coins. "Embolism..." he murmured. The gendarmes were fools, but the doctor, he would see the truth...

Léon's right fist loosened, and a coin rolled into the gutter.

A ten-cent piece! Léon dropped to his knees and felt around for the errant piece of change. He could not find it; he was nowhere near.

"There! By your feet!" called out a ferret-faced boy.

At his feet, Léon found a five-cent piece. "I could have sworn it was ten," he muttered. He pocketed the coin and continued down the slope. He was in a daze.

## 2. CNK

The matter was both admirably simple and damnably confusing.

It was all Vega's fault. Vega was the Petitquartiers' resident skeleton. More specifically, a skeletal dog. Wasting away, condemned by the veterinarian, the animal was quite literally dying on its feet. Finishing her off would be an act of mercy. The previous day, the Petitquartiers had finally decided to do it. And Léon was in charge of the operation.

First thing that morning, therefore, he had climbed up to the first floor, to his entomologist father's laboratory. The old man had left for Paris at dawn. In truth, M. Paul Petitquartier was only an entomologist in the broadest sense of the term. This kind and gentle little man was only interested in spiders. He pursued them obsessively, going so far as to keep the attic in a repulsive state of filth to lure them in—at which he succeeded admirably. Once he had captured them, he subjected the critters to cyanide vapors and sealed them in glass jars. Using this method, he'd amassed a considerable collection. Each little monster was stored individually, with a label bearing the date of its capture (nobody knew why) in a cupboard that was out of bounds to everyone save M. Petitquartier himself. Madame Petitquartier protested in vain. It was no use. M. Petitquartier was willing to make concessions in every part of his life except for one: his arachnids. One of the amateur entomologist's greatest pleasures in life was to study his specimens through a magnifying glass for hours on end. He seemed to take unhealthy delight in examining each hairy body with its tangle of legs.

Naturally, Léon went straight to the forbidden room and discovered a glass vial three-quarters full of a gray powder, bearing on its label the chemical formula: CNK. Below this, mentioned almost in passing, it read: POTASSIUM CYANIDE. POISON.

Perfect, thought Léon.

He took the vial.

Downstairs in the pâtisserie, he took a honey tartlet and conscientiously sprinkled it with the poison. Then he headed out through the kitchen and into the courtyard which led to the street, where Vega's kennel was situated. The dog lay on the pavement; a thin bundle who looked as though her bones might puncture her side at any moment.

But just as Léon was about to serve the treat to the unfortunate creature, he experienced a strange melancholy sensation. He needed a moment. He returned to the kitchen, placing the tartlet on the table while he pulled himself together.

When he looked back, the tartlet was gone.

He peered under chairs, he ransacked cupboards, he used a broom to poke and prod beneath furniture. The only things this turned up were errant corks, nuts, dead flies, spiders still entangled in their webs. (Not a bad haul, his father might have said.) But no tartlet. Initially, Léon cursed his poor eyesight. Then he headed through to the pâtisserie itself: his mother hadn't touched anything. He went through to the adjoining kitchen: Justin, the baker, yawned and agreed to help with the search. A few moments later, Léon heard suspicious noises from the courtyard. He bolted out and caught Justin with two fingers down his throat, desperately forcing himself to vomit. Sheepishly, Justin admitted that this morning—as well as every other morning, for that matter—he'd pinched one of Madame Petitquartier's cakes.

He didn't think it was a tartlet, but all the same, better safe than sorry....

"Don't be stupid," Léon said. "If you'd had the cyanide, you'd be dead already. Stiff as a board by now."

The investigation resumed. Madame Anna Petitquartier, a plump, mustachioed woman, flapped her short arms and clucked like an angry hen as she fluttered from one room to another. All in vain.

To be on the safe side, Léon headed out into the courtyard. After all, anyone could have approached from the street. A kid, maybe... But the street was deserted. Shutters closed, doors locked, the street was still asleep, or at least in the process of waking up, yawning, stretching, and reflecting on what a wonderful thing Sundays were.

It seemed that the only living creature in that quiet town was a gypsy in a white cap, navy blue sweater, and espadrilles. He darted across the street and away with cat-like speed.

Madame Petitquarter cried out: "Hélène! She must have taken the tartlet! She'll have got it mixed up with the cakes she has to deliver in town!" (The silly goose Hélène worked for the Petitquartiers as an assistant in the pâtisserie.)

Léon and Justin rushed off, leaving Madame Petitquartier on duty behind the counter, frantically wringing her greasy hands.

They knew where Hélène was heading; they caught up with her swiftly and told her what was going on. The little fool immediately burst into tears and cried: "Leave me alone! Let me go! Let me go!"

Léon demanded: "Why? What's going on?"

At that, Hélène admitted that this morning... Just this morning? Well... this morning... and a few other mornings... she'd pinched a few cakes to give to her dear mother. They let her go, and she ran. It might not be too late!

Now it was a matter of going door to door, visiting all the houses where Hélène had made a delivery. They told each customer a tale about spoiled flour and less-than-fresh eggs. Most were bemused, and some incredulous. One even seized a newly delivered tartlet and bit into it. Instead of dropping dead, the fellow just said: "Tastes all right to me!"

Back at the pâtisserie, Madame Petitquartier examined her pastries suspiciously. She could scarcely bring herself to sell any of them, and even tried to talk customers out of making a purchase. Unfortunately, this brought out the worst in certain local contrarians, who insisted on buying even more.

Finally, Justin and Léon reappeared.

Madame Petitquartier was once again assailed by doubt. "Are you *sure* it was a tartlet?"

"Yes," answered her son definitively.

"All right, all right," said his mother, "I just thought you might have got it wrong, that's all. Are you sure it wasn't a piece of flan? All right, no need to look at me like that! We all make mistakes from time to time. And what about this poison? It might have scattered everywhere, I suppose?"

That was when Léon, exasperated, went out. He headed for the place Biancour, to the café, to await the announcement of a misfortune which he now knew to be inevitable.

*

That was at half past seven. An hour later, he learned of Pipo's death. And so the problem was solved: the prowler who had pinched the tartlet was the Italian.

At about the same time, a gypsy entering town via la porte Bardoul had reached the place Biancour. He was the second one Léon had seen that morning; the second since the beginning of this unfortunate affair.

And now, Léon was marching back along rue Ludovic-Petau-de-Maulette, which he had already traversed twice that morning. This time, he was heading toward the valley. He was going to l'Étang de la Ville.

At place Lebreton, he encountered another gypsy.

He slowed his pace. *C...N...K... C...N...K... C...N...K...* he chanted softly. These three letters gave rhythm to each step. In his mind's eye he glimpsed the inscription: POISON. Sometimes the image of a hideous hairy spider reared in his imagination.

Along rue de la Moutière, Léon encountered another gypsy.

Soon he was out in the country. He began to pick up speed. Somewhere out there, among the shards of bottles and old cans, was he going to discover the secret of Pipo's death? Pipo who, in his lifetime, had lived in a run-down wooden shack at the end of rue Quesnay, on the edge of town... Pipo, known to his Italian friends as Pipello, Pipellito, Pipellinello, Pipellinellito; and to the French as "Pipe Head" or "The Pipe Man."

Pipo—the darts players had already got him dead and buried. For him, the game was over.

Houdini—whose real name was Auguste Bonnaud—gave an excellent imitation of a man with St. Vitus' Dance and then, carelessly rubbing his forehead, produced three billiard balls from thin air, to the immense bewilderment of the landlord, who thought he had hidden them pretty well. He did not care for Houdini's tricks, and grabbed the three balls, weighed them suspiciously in his hands, before stowing them under lock and key in a drawer.

In the square, children who had never examined a Mercedes before, but who had "seen plenty of others"; little know-it-alls, versed in all things mechanical, prowled around the sparkling automobile, prodding a tire here, a headlamp there, testing the bumper, exchanging appreciative remarks and criticisms in language of perfect technical precision.

All over town, there came the creak of pumps and the clatter of garbage cans. Wheels rattled over cobble-stones. The town's well-to-do were at last beginning to surface, in dressing gown and slippers, or camisole and curlers, to open their shutters, to take a breath of morning air, to turn on their bath taps, to open a razor while reflecting idly on the death of Louis XVI, to open a jar of beauty cream. Even the deepest sleepers were now up and about, some having cleverly awoken at the most seductive part of their dreams, in the secret hope that it would make it easier to pick up where they left off come nightfall.

Between the two buses, the Mercedes, its blue fenders looking like outstretched wings, suggested the absurd image of a dragonfly pinned between a pair of bats.

There were now four gypsies in the place Biancour.

A quarter of an hour later, there were eight.

### 3. THE SILENT WALKER

A kilometer from Montfort, a hundred meters from an isolated farmhouse where agricultural machinery, bits of old carts, and barrels loomed ruminatively in a desolate yard, stretched a body of murky water, swathed in a robe of moss and decomposing leaves, and choked with diseased rushes. Strictly speaking, this lake had no specific outline, instead stretching out in all directions and turning gradually to muddy slush which lapped at the surrounding grasslands. This was l'Étang-la-Ville.

It was surrounded by the pitiful ruins of a barbed wire fence, which served no discernible purpose. A short distance away— just across the street, in fact—was a heap of manure, piled with old newspapers, broken bottles and general household refuse. A haven for blowflies.

It was there, in the midst of the trash heap, among the fermenting straw and gleeful insects, that Pipo, the laborer from l'Ouest-Lumière, had come to die. What was he doing out here so early? Perhaps it was the simple desire for a bicycle ride in the cool morning air... After all, it was early July; the night had been a humid one.

When he came in sight of l'Étang, Léon was surprised to find the spot deserted. He had expected to find a crowd of onlookers.

A weird feeling came over him. It was not simply emotion; it was more complex and subtle, indefinable. A vague tingle of menace in the atmosphere that was already leaden with summer heat. The countryside was perfectly silent; the tree-bordered path empty; the pond drowsy; the woods dead. Too silent, too empty, too drowsy...

His inspection of the trash heap and the sardine cans took no longer than five minutes. No hint of a tartlet, not a scrap, not even the tiniest crumb. Of course not. Between a couple of empty crab cans (each now populated by obscenely bloated blowflies), a brand-new spare valve gleamed. It must have rolled out of Pipo's satchel when he collapsed. It still had its cover, which Léon unscrewed. Underneath was the usual little piston, which seemed to work perfectly. Léon prodded it with his index finger. In short, a perfectly good valve. Léon slipped it into his pocket.

A breeze was moving in from the west. If only it would rain, Léon thought with a sigh, twitching his nostrils at the ephemeral breath of air. "Weird," he said aloud. He was not speaking of the breeze, or of the potential for rain. Not even the valve. Without fully understanding, Léon was already beginning to perceive the origin of that dull, almost electrical tingle he had felt a moment ago when entering this suspiciously still landscape.

And the odd thing was not that he hadn't discovered the tartlet, but rather the fact (which he only realized now) that he had felt the presentiment—not just a presentiment: a certainty!—that he would *not* discover it. And of course he had not discovered it. But why, "of course"?

Léon craned his neck. On the other side of l'Étang, a man was pushing his way through the crisscrossed branches toward the path. Tall and broad, with one beady eye, the other a dark hollow in a face the color of bricks. Blue sweater, white pants, cap, espadrilles: a gypsy. Without so much as a glance in the teenager's direction, the man passed by.

For a moment, standing atop the trash heap, the pastry chef's son gazed at this vast silhouette as it dwindled in the distance, traipsing silently along the opposite side of the road. It was only after the gypsy had disappeared that Léon Petitquartier decided to go back to Montfort. This time he didn't take the tree-lined lane, but a narrow, steep-sided path bordered by bramble hedges and fringed with rust-spotted leaves.

When Léon got back to place Biancour, he learned from one of the bus drivers that two gypsies—one male and one female—had just been found dead in their caravan, on the main road, not far from the Hostellerie de la Duchesse Anne. Poisonous mushrooms, or so it seemed.

### 4. THE GYPSIES

Montfort was now swarming with gypsies. Never had the place seen so many. The fleet of caravans on the way into town resembled a monstrous green and yellow snake. They brought with them a range of attractions for Bastille Day, July 14th, including a circus. They had set up camp on a barren patch of land, hammering their tent pegs into the dry earth. At mealtimes, animalistic roars emerged from the three tallest and—it was to be hoped—most secure caravans. The roar of large felines, the yelp of monkeys, the bleating of intelligent goats, the yaps of tightrope-walking pugs. And of course there were the placid, majestic shire-horses which pulled all those wagons. A grizzly bear, chained to a stone trough, paced impatiently. From time to time he brandished a threatening paw. Alas, this bear, which had evidently been a handsome beast once upon a time, had now lost most of his splendor along with his fur, which was coming out in clumps at a rate of one handful per hour. This towering carnivore had the air of an old gentleman who has fallen on hard times, some Russian grand duke who has descended into poverty but who nevertheless makes an effort to keep up appearances, and whose once-sumptuous fur coat is now irreparably moth-eaten.

The bear was known as Nicolas; apt for a duke. But the gypsy children, who had less sophisticated tastes, knew his real name was Martin.

In many ways, it was a sad menagerie. There was a simple-minded elephant, bound unceremoniously by the leg, which scratched its rump enthusiastically against the trunk of a nearby tree. These efforts had caused the creature's skin to develop an infection which would eventually prove fatal.

Smoke plumed overhead, cauldrons clattered: dinner was being prepared. The aroma drifted into town on the breeze.

The streets of Montfort were now crowded with people waiting for the festivities to begin; individuals whose colorful garb belied their hardiness and sheer physical strength.

And now two of them were dead, killed by poison that very morning.

Léon Petitquartier darted down rue Ludovic-Petau-de-Maulette like a fleeing rat.

"The best thing I could do," he suggested to his mother, "would be to go to the police. To make a statement."

"Never!" said Mme. Petitquartier. "For one thing, the business would be ruined."

"All right, whatever you say. But I'm going into town. I want to see what's going on."

Two mounted policemen stood in the place Biancour. They had, in fact, dismounted. They were examining the splendid Mercedes, neither man saying a word. While most people (those who are not gendarmes) enjoy a chat, these two enjoyed their silence. Their two silences echoed each other marvelously, betokening mutual respect. That silence carried the weight of knowledge of two men who had seen everything, who had plumbed the darkest depths of the human heart.

They were silent not because they had nothing to say to each other, but because, after careful examination, they were in total agreement on everything. And so acute was the physical similarity between them that it seemed there was only one gendarme on Place Biancour, standing before a vast mirror. A lone policeman, utterly in tune with himself. And their two mounts looked to be a single horse. The policeman and his reflection, as well as his horse and the horse's reflection, were in perfect agreement on all matters.

Léon approached. "How's it going?"

"Not bad."

"Would either of you gentlemen care for a drink with me?"

The two men answered as one: "Sorry, Petitquartier. Not today. Busy, busy, busy."

And they mounted their horses once more, saluted, then trotted off along rue Amaury.

So they don't want to be seen drinking with me by daylight? Léon thought. All right: the hell with them! He circled the Mercedes for a moment, then entered the café and for the first time in his life he ordered a Pernod.

"Make it two."

Léon turned. A gypsy had appeared from nowhere, as though springing from between the cobble-stones themselves, and followed him into the bar. The gypsy, sensing Léon's eyes on him, stared back at the boy and bared his white teeth—teeth which seemed all the whiter against his sun-burnished skin.

With lightning speed, Léon realized what was going on. Not only had two gypsies been poisoned by the cyanide-laced tartlet; the *other gypsies knew about it*. They were following Léon. They were watching him. Everywhere he went, he ran into them. Place Biancourt, rue Petau, rue de la Moutiere, place Lebreton. Everywhere. And there was even one of them lurking out by l'Étang-la-Ville! He had been watching, too. Spying. No doubt he had been on Léon's tail ever since he left the pâtisserie.

Léon raised his glass to his lips. But he was not destined to taste his first Pernod that day. At the entrance to the rue Ludovic-Petau-de-Maulette, he glimpsed a stout figure. Thanks to his long-sightedness, Léon was better equipped to recognize a distant figure than a near one. He had to rely on his other senses to keep from running into things. But he would have known those footsteps anywhere: it was Justin, the baker.

He was peering around nervously. Sensing something afoot, Léon headed out to join him. The gypsy downed his Pernod, dropped a couple of coins on the counter and promptly vanished.

"Watch out," Justin whispered to his employer's son with a somewhat ridiculous air of mystery. "Be careful. There were two of them over on rue Petau. Two gypsies. They had a goat with them, would you believe it? They went into the pâtisserie and were nosing about the place. In the end they bought a chocolate éclair, took it out onto the doorstep and—guess what?—they fed it to the goat! Can you imagine? And what's more, the goat ate it! Then a few more of them came along. So your mother sent me to find you. There's something very fishy going on. Very fishy indeed. Léon—I think they know how their friends got poisoned."

"But Justin, I thought it was something to do with poisoned mushrooms...?"

"Pfffttt!" said Justin, flapping his hand as though to discourage an unwelcome gnat. "Just rumors. What does that prove? Suppose they made up that story to keep the police out of their business? Maybe they even fricasseed a few poisoned mushrooms to make it more convincing? Take it from me, Léon, these people like to handle these things on their own terms. Be very careful, do you hear? I don't like this one bit...."

Although Léon Petitquartier didn't have much in the way

of a sense of humor, the almost farcically tragic attitude of the
baker might have brought a smile to his lips if, at that moment,
he had not noticed from the corner of his eye a group of five
gypsies watching him from the corner of rue de Sance. A shiver
rippled down his spine. Justin frowned, then said: "Come on."

They headed off in the opposite direction.

In the square, two horns sounded. Crammed with their human
cargo destined for the 10.59 train, the buses moved off in the
direction of the station, leaving the Mercedes alone once more.

In the café, an obsessive and solitary darts player aimed for
the bullseye and missed.

## 5. THE SPOTTED BRAMBLE LEAF

Back at the bakery: "Well?" Léon asked.

"Well what? Justin already told you! There were two of them
in here, with a goat. What are we going to do?"

Léon tried to calm his mother. "Come on now, don't panic!
It was most likely a coincidence. They were taking the goat for
a walk."

"Maybe that stuff wasn't poison after all?" Hélène suggested.
"Just snake oil or something?"

"You may be onto something!" said Léon. "Let's find out."

Under the strict supervision of his mother, Justin, and Hélène,
Léon sprinkled some of the powder onto a piece of meat which
he took into the courtyard and placed a couple of inches from
Vega's muzzle. The dog craned her neck and stuck out her
tongue. What happened next was instantaneous. She stiffened
in a brief but violent convulsion, then rolled over. Out of her
misery at last.

Hélène let out a stifled sob. A heavy silence ensued. Justin
broke it: "Well, well," he said.

Grabbing the deceased dog by a paw, he dragged her behind
the kennel and then came back for a shovel. "I'm going to dig
a hole," he said.

Mme Petitquartier returned to the kitchen. Hélène went
shopping. Justin was serving his function as an impromptu
gravedigger. So Léon returned to his search for the tartlet. But
still he could not find it. However, he *did* find something in
the pâtisserie, close to the front door: a bramble leaf, peppered
with rust. This disturbed him greatly. It recalled to his mind the

bramble-lined path where he had observed that curious fellow out by l'Étang-la-Ville....

Léon had heard many tales of gypsy vengeance. He knew that seemingly innocuous artifacts could take on sinister significance. Did the leaf mean: *You have been spotted? Marked for death?* The leaf had obviously been plucked from its tree that morning; it was not yet withered. The rusty marks were a deep scarlet. The color of blood.

"What have you got there?" his mother asked.

"Nothing, Ma. Just a bramble leaf."

Mme. Petitquartier shrugged. "Come on. It's lunchtime."

## 6. THE CLOCKWORK MAN

It was noon. Justin and Hélène had left. In the pâtisserie kitchen, facing each other across a yellow-and-white checked tablecloth, Mme. Petitquartier and her son ate a quick lunch. What could they have said to one another? They had both tackled the problem to the best of their ability, coming up with theories that were just crazy enough to be the truth. And they were no closer to establishing how the tartlet had vanished. That morning there had been three sudden deaths in Montfort. Were there more to come? Nothing was impossible. They both tried hard not to think about it.

"Eat something, Léon. Have some cold veal."

"No thanks, Ma."

"All right—tomato salad. It's good; very refreshing."

"I'd rather have the cyanide, thanks."

\*

The cool breeze which had swept through town that morning was now gone. In its place was a torpid, despondent humidity. Outside all of Montfort's cafés sat languid diners with cold meats and salads in front of them. Their conversation was accompanied by a perpetual hum of flies buzzing around mayonnaise jars, liquor glasses, sugar cubes and cakes.

"Let me make you a nice strong coffee, dear. It will keep your strength up."

"Good idea, Ma."

From the place Biancour came horrifying screams.

"What's that? What's happening?" Mme. Petitquartier demanded, frozen in terror at the coffee grinder.

"Nothing, Ma. Kids, most likely."

It was indeed kids, running rings around the parked buses while an exasperated conductor chased them, flapping his handkerchief as though to dispel flies from his dinner table.

By one in the afternoon, the town of Montfort was supping cold drinks, licking ice creams, removing its collar, unbuttoning its waistcoat, and fanning itself with old magazines. It said things like "Dear God, I'm dying," or "Lord! This heat is unbearable."

At place Biancour, the Mercedes was once again alone. Like great lumbering bovines, the two buses had gone back to the station for their ration of oil, gasoline and water. Perhaps, somewhere in their metallic hearts, they felt guilty about leaving that pretty little car all alone, unchaperoned....

The two drivers stood by their respective vehicles, one foot planted firmly on the running board, smoking cigarettes and chatting amiably while they waited for the train to roll in, and for its conductor to croon a familiar ditty: "Montfort! Montfort! Montfort!"

Neatly folding his napkin, Léon said: "I'm going out."

He wanted to go to the gypsy camp, without really knowing what to do there. He just felt a need to roam among the tents and caravans.

So he put on his Panama hat and took a short cut along the rue de Paris, past the Hostellerie de la Duchesse Anne, beyond the sports fields, and there it was—the camp.

As he approached the cluster of caravans, Léon saw several women and children going about their business. The kids were playing; a boy was doing cartwheels while others were squealing and bickering. Still others were methodically rummaging through heaps of stones, as though searching for buried treasure.

They were in fact looking for round pebbles, which they proceeded to hurl with startling vigor.

The women were busy with domestic chores. Occasionally, one of them would burst into song in an astonishingly pure voice; a voice which dwindled into silence as swiftly as it had arisen, and sounded to Léon's ears like the sentimental, dreamy murmur of the grasslands themselves.

The heat continued to rise. The fields were listless, but that did not stop the gypsy women from picking handfuls of alfalfa and clover. Others were scouring basins, wringing out freshly-washed clothes, or else hanging them to dry from long ropes.

Others were bathing very small children. The men must all be in town wetting their whistle, or else dozing somewhere.

Surrounded by these industrious women who did not hesitate to stare at him, and these children who galloped around him as though he were invisible—and fearing he might be on the receiving end of one of their pebbles—Léon was overwhelmed by a sudden wave of despair. The enigma of the missing tartlet seemed more impenetrable than ever.

What was he hoping to discover here? Was he hoping to solve the mystery of the two dead gypsies? How was he even going to find their caravan among all these others? What was there to set it apart from the crowd? There were more than twenty of them, all perfectly alike. The same color scheme, the same doors at the top of four wooden steps, the same windows. Completely identical in every way.

As Léon stood there, studying the caravans indecisively, a lanky figure appeared, like a puppet or a demon, in the doorway of one of these caravans and leapt to the ground. He was swinging a flexible metallic object, the nature of which Léon could not determine, thanks to his poor eyesight. It looked like some kind of oversized spring. Carefully twisting it to his satisfaction, the fellow then removed a box from within a metal bucket that no doubt served him as a toolbox. This box, also metallic, was round, riddled with holes and serrated. He placed the mainspring inside the box, which looked to contain some sort of crude clockwork mechanism, then adjusted a few pins before running a chain around the serrated case.

Next, he picked another metal box out of the bucket—this one larger than the first. He slipped the first box into the second, and secured it in place. On one of the faces of the large square box was a hollow tube, a kind of cannon, into which the gypsy now plunged an iron rod shaped like a key. He twisted the key two or three times, and the apparatus issued a loud report which startled Léon.

The gypsy smiled and approached Léon. "You like that, boy? What do you say, you and I take a walk?"

Léon did not answer; he could not take his eyes off the mechanical device.

"You see," the gypsy continued, hefting the device in his palm, "I make toys to keep myself occupied."

With that, he leapt back into the caravan, leaving Léon more disturbed and confused than ever.

Curling his lip as Justin had, the teenager repeated the words the baker had used over at place Biancour: "I don't like this one bit...."

Following a steep path which took him between a wall and a barbed wire fence, he headed on towards the nearby château.

He had scarcely travelled a hundred meters when something whizzed past his ear, making him jump. Somewhere ahead, a pebble clattered to the ground. Léon picked up his pace.

## 7. CHÂTEAU OF SECRETS

Five minutes later, the pastry chef's son reached the foot of the hill leading up to the château. A veritable eagle's nest, according to the tourist guides. In fact, however powerful the historical interest of these eleventh century ruins might be, what makes the place especially attractive is the abundance of vegetation which thrives there. Visitors may wander for hours along a tangle of winding paths; paths which meander up and down, which occasionally cross a delightful little bridge whose sole raison d'être seems to be the idyllic wonderment it evinces in the observer. Nettle-lined paths peppered with ladybirds, holly-laden paths punctuated by yellow snails, paths lined with hazel trees and bedecked with cobwebs. Unspoiled trails, bathed in shade, dense with foliage, which give the impression of wandering in a secret garden, far away from the real world.

But the real world is not far away at all.

There are names. Lovers' names, etched into wood and stone. It is like a blissful alien planet where love alone holds sway.

They are everywhere, carved with the point of ardent penknives; on the plinth supporting a statue of M. Adolphe de Dion, not to mention the ruins themselves, these immutable letters affirm immortal passions. Hearts are skewered by arrows. This love will last forever.

Along this path, these amorous couples are unavoidable. Beneath the statue of M. Adolphe de Dion, Alphonsine and Charles. They love each other. On the little bridge, Octave and Henriette. They love each other too. At the very top of the tower, Jean and Louise: lovers for life.

That day, though, Léon found the location oddly bereft of

lovers. The excessive heat, no doubt, had put them off. Léon took the opportunity to lie down in the shade of the tower, just to catch his breath and gather his thoughts for a moment. Almost immediately, exhaustion washed over him and he collapsed into a heavy yet troubled sleep, assailed by dreams of phantom gypsies in espadrilles. A few feet away, a notice put in place by the local municipality read: TRESPASSERS WILL BE PROSECUTED.

Léon had been dozing for perhaps a quarter of an hour when a strange tingling sensation in his face woke him. Running his fingers over his cheeks, he realized he had been sprinkled with gravel. *The tower! The tower's crumbling away to nothing!* he thought. He cast his blurry eyes upward and saw, dangling over the uppermost edge of the tower, a pair of feet. Before he could recover from his surprise, the feet swiftly withdrew and disappeared.

An instant later, a man appeared, descending the tower steps, rubbing his hands white with saltpeter. He smiled at Léon and then, without a sound, headed off along the path.

An instant later, Léon Petitquartier was marching along a different path, heading towards the valley. Pushing aside spindly branches that seemed to claw at him, he convinced himself he could hear whispers from the nearby thicket. An illusion, it had to be; just the sound of blood throbbing in his temples. But soon the illusion was dispelled, when he heard an echo of laughter, and the snap of a branch underfoot. The gypsies! They were following him every step of the way.

His heart pounding, but still striving to maintain a calm outward demeanor, he carried on for another hundred meters or so, then stopped and listened. Nothing. Silence.

In the distance came the sound of two horns: the buses, heading for the 2.27 train.

A little further on, Léon discerned a silhouette among the trees, a cap-wearing gypsy holding some sort of mechanical device up to his eye, peering through a viewfinder... the clockwork man from the camp!

The machine issued a soft 'click' and the stranger—who was in fact just an ordinary tourist—wedged his Kodak under his armpit and went off in search of other picturesque panoramas.

Léon headed back the way he had come. He crossed the little bridge where Octave and Henriette came to whisper their sweet secrets.

He glanced down, and glimpsed another gypsy below, staring up at him.

Léon pressed on. Yet another gypsy watched him from a nearby tree. About a hundred meters further, on a path lined with lime trees, he spotted two more of them, sitting at the foot of the statue of M. Adolphe de Dion, where Octave the gravedigger's son, and Henriette, who worked at the Nouvelles Galeries, had scratched their undying oaths into the stone; oaths which were beyond their power to fulfil. This place, where so many couples before them had come to declare a love that would last forever—in the loosest sense of the word.

When they spotted Léon, the two gypsies did not move. They did not even blink. Léon found this disturbing. Their apparent indifference chilled him even more than an overt threat would have. Why did these two men pretend to go on chatting instead of launching their attack? Why hadn't the man in the ruins, the man beneath the bridge, or the man in the tree taken the initiative and plunged a stiletto blade into his heart?

Léon was now consumed by a fear worsened by its unending nature. The nerves of this unfortunate student of the École Pigier were in tatters. He prickled with goosebumps, rippling like a thousand ball-bearings beneath his skin.

Each bend in the path brought more lurking apparitions in espadrilles. How many could there possibly be? Fifty? Or perhaps just three or four, gifted with the supernatural power of being in multiple places at once? Behind each hedge, a gypsy. Behind every tree trunk, a gypsy. The sound of rustling branches? Well, that was a trio of gypsies pressing on past a linden, or an acacia, or a chestnut tree. A disembodied head materialized on the ground—a phantom? Hardly; just another gypsy, the "snakeman" from the carnival, practicing his moves. In short, they were everywhere. This forest was a haunted phantasmagoria of tightrope walkers and bloodthirsty acrobats.

But they disappeared as swiftly as they had materialized. No sooner had he glimpsed them than they vanished into thin air.

At long last, Léon reached the edge of the wood. He spotted the cemetery wall, then the first few houses, then the first tangibly human figures. He was back in the outskirts of town, on his way back to the world he knew.

In the distance, he heard the pounding of a drum. The town crier? Léon quickened his pace. No sooner had he reached the place Biancour than he heard the man with the bass drum calling his name.

"It was you, was it, Petitquartier, who put this poisoned cake into circulation?"

Having said his piece, the town crier hoisted up his drum and headed off to another corner of Montfort to spread his alarming message: "Attention! This morning a tartlet was stolen...."

## 8. THE PHANTOM TARTLET

So Justin hadn't been able to keep his mouth shut.

The poisoned tartlet was causing shock waves throughout the town. Ten people had already visited Mme. Petitquartier's pâtisserie, not to buy but to vehemently recriminate. The fact that these people were still perfectly alive and healthy—and therefore had not even come close to the poison—did not seem to matter.

By the grace of God they were not dead, but that was not the point—they *could* have died, *that* was the point! And the fact that they had not was no thanks to the Petitquartiers...

Everyone who had eaten a tartlet that morning now felt a retrospective horror of impending mortality. For those who had *not* eaten a tartlet, it was even worse.

"What about the gendarmes?" Léon asked his mother.

"They came by," said Mme Petitquartier. "I told them everything. What else could I do?"

Léon headed over to the gendarmerie himself, where he explained the complicated history of the tartlet in detail. They gave him a severe telling-off for trying to keep the matter a secret, it was sheer luck that a disaster had not occurred....

"What do you mean, 'hasn't occurred'? What about Pipo? And the two gypsies?"

"Don't be stupid. Pipo died of an embolism, and the gypsies died from eating poisoned mushrooms."

There might still be hope, thought Léon. If there were no more deaths by nightfall, they might be safe. Thanks to the interminable heat, the tartlet would be completely inedible by the following day.

By three o'clock that afternoon, the local gossips had turned the honey tartlet into an apricot tart.

By half-past, it was an éclair.

By 3.45, you could take your pick of apricot, plum, quince, raspberry, rhubarb, pineapple, almond, flan, èclair, cornet, cream puff, apple turnover, galette... The tartlet was now a nebulous beast, a shapeshifter. The poison was everywhere.

One by one, all the pâtisseries in town closed their doors. The general watchword was, *Don't touch the cakes!*

But it was not just cakes.

Pralines, chocolate drops, and other confections were hurled into the gutter as well, just to be on the safe side. Smokers rid themselves of their tobacco. Chewers got rid of their gum. It was not worth the risk, they thought.

At ten past five, the buses returned from the station with the passengers from the 4.48 train. And they had sensational news. Two signalmen at the station, a pair of brothers, had found themselves afflicted with diarrhea—but not just any diarrhea, this was bright blue! What's more, one of the foremen at the Ouest-Lumière electric company had not been seen since noon, when he went off on his lunch break.

Almost immediately, however, it turned out that a gluttonous overconsumption of beans had led to the signalmen's disgrace, while the Ouest-Lumière foreman was soon found in a quiet corner, drunk out of his mind.

At these latest developments, certain heartless citizens could not help but laugh. This provoked indignation in others, and ultimately a sense of Christian beneficence.

But the number of people who found the situation hilarious soon began to grow—the laughter spread with distressing rapidity.

Before long, it was everywhere. Initially isolated, these individuals now snickered together with abandon. The laughter continued to gather momentum, spreading like an epidemic. Soon the mass hysteria of maniacal laughter was getting out of hand.

By six o'clock, the entire town had succumbed.

This tartlet business was just about the funniest thing that had ever happened. People slapped their thighs and sang songs about it; *Have You Seen the Tartlet?* was a particular favorite, sung to the tune of "La Cap du père Bugeaud."

Comedians approached people on café terraces, bearing baskets of macarons and wafers: "Tartlets! Get your tartlets here! Guaranteed pure potassium cyanide, ask for the Cyanide Special!"

The Cyanide Special proved a hit. Boys came round with powdered sugar: "Pinch of cyanide, sir? Perfect for nourishing the blood, and strengthening the bones. Highly recommended by the Medical Corps!"

Yet more wags enjoyed a moment in the spotlight thanks to their sudden grimaces and eye-rolls, before a dramatic collapse accompanied by a bird-like squawk. These numerous death scenes attracted much deserved applause. The town of Montfort could scarcely contain its delight. The place positively writhed with demented glee.

Place Biancour was even better. A fellow displayed a cardboard box containing six real-life tartlets. To procure them, he'd been obliged to hammer for an hour on the shutters of a closed pâtisserie, threatening to smash their windows if they wouldn't serve him. Now, he sat down triumphantly with his tartlets.

"Nobody wants to share them with me? Well, it's your loss! See: I have a trick."

The crowd which had gathered around him stared at the tartlets, which were now covered with flies. Sensing a decent joke, they waited for the punch line.

Suddenly, the man swept the flies away with the back of his hand, then seized one tartlet after another and devoured them whole. Then he ordered a white wine.

"I'll let you in on the secret. I leave my tartlets in the sun. I wait five minutes for the flies to have their fill. And if it doesn't kill *them*, why should it kill *me*?"

Delirium. People cheered for their new hero. A group of youngsters lit lanterns and undertook a torchlit procession in his honor. And the man himself enjoyed a period of stardom. A month later, he was still affectionately known as "*Monsieur les Mouches.*"

By eight o'clock, the crowds began to disperse. They were still cheerful, but the laughter had ceased. Indeed, their sides were beginning to ache from the non-stop mirth.

By nine o'clock, fatigue had set in.

Ten o'clock: to bed, to bed. Lights went out, one by one at first, then in twos, fours, sixes. Clusters of twinkling stars, suddenly snuffed out. The occupants of the gypsy caravans also readied themselves for bed. Night had fallen. A gently rustling night, as though accompanied by softly slithering tendrils.

Apart from a few boozers in the backrooms of bars (who went largely ignored), nobody thought of the tartlet.

Midnight. If anyone thought of the tartlet now, it was only in the distant vagaries of a dream.

From the dimly lit streets and alleys, there now came movement; a lively yet furtive bustle. Claws on pavement, grunts, yaps. The gutters and garbage cans were now overflowing with treasures!

The dogs, the cats, and the rats commenced their feast.

That was when the sudden sound of galloping footsteps in rue Amaury shattered the nocturnal calm.

Then, from place Biancour, the rumble of an engine. The Mercedes, on the move at last?

It was!

But the sleek automobile had scarcely turned onto the square when the two gendarmes who, that very afternoon, had disdained to drink with Petitquartier ("busy, busy, busy"), sprang from the shadows.

"Halt! Halt or we fire!"

Rather than heeding these instructions, the driver of the Mercedes accelerated. The lawmen fired low, and a lucky shot punctured a tire. The vehicle carried on at speed, only to swerve and smash straight into a wall, where it came to a juddering halt. A single headlight seemed to wink in the darkness.

The driver was handcuffed. He was in fact a "gentleman thief," a cat burglar, who had spent the entire day hiding in an attic, just waiting for nightfall. His patience had apparently paid off; he had cracked the safe and his pockets were now swollen with banknotes and jewels.

The gendarmes took him away.

## 9. THE LAST BUS

Only one bus went out to pick up arrivals from the 12:30 train. In fact, there was just a single passenger; a thin, stooped figure, who climbed into the back of the bus and slumped into a seat. Evidently exhausted, he was soon dozing with his mouth wide open.

The traveler got out at place Biancour, handed thirty sous

to the driver, then ambled with a spidery gait into the darkness of rue Ludovic-Petau-de-Maulette.

"Isn't that Petitquartier? Aren't you going to tell him what's happened?"

"Quiet! It's none of our business. Come on, we've still got time for a nightcap...."

The only light in rue Ludovic-Petau-de-Maulette came from the pâtisserie. It seeped through the glass door, bathing Vega's kennel in a warm glow.

"Ah! Somebody's still awake!"

Indeed somebody was. Both mother and son were waiting for him at the kitchen table. M. Petitquartier entered the shop and collapsed into the nearest chair.

"I'm back!" he yawned.

Léon stood. "Dad, there's something I have to tell you...."

But his mother stopped him. "Let me, Léon."

Léon sat back down.

"Paul, something awful has happened."

"What?" M. Petitquartier mumbled, half-asleep.

"Léon left a tartlet on the table."

"There!" said Léon, slapping a corner of the table. "There. About half-past six this morning..."

"So?" his father wanted to know.

"So, I looked away for a second, and when I looked back it was gone!"

With an effort, Léon's father got to his feet again. "Gone..." He smiled. "Well, these things happen, I suppose. Could be worse." He began to undo a package he had brought back from Paris.

"Yes," said his son, marching agitatedly toward the fireplace, "yes, but..."

He handed the vial of gray powder to his father, turning it to reveal the label: CNK. POISON.

"It was meant for Vega," he concluded.

"What? *What?*" his father stammered. "My cyanide? You put my cyanide on..."

Léon nodded.

"I see," M. Petitquartier whispered. "Well, I was the one who took the tartlet."

"What!" his wife shrieked. "What did you do with it? Who did you give it to?"

"No one. I ate it."

For the first time in his life, Léon permitted himself a loud and disrespectful exclamation.

"It must be the reaction...." murmured M. Petitquartier.

"Of course it's the reaction, but what are we going to *do*...?"

And then, something even more surprising happened. Just as his son had allowed himself a moment's irreverence, the meek and gentle M. Petitquartier lost his temper. "Foolish boy! You don't understand! You don't understand at all! I'm talking about *Kilini's Reaction*."

The bemused look exchanged by Léon and his mother caused the collector of arachnids to pull himself together posthaste.

"I'm sorry. I let myself get carried away. But what I'm trying to say is that there's nothing to worry about. Of course, you don't know about Bougault and Perrier, or Saint-Rat and the others, do you? Alas, nobody does these days... Anyway, these great scientists discovered that the sugar in fruit, honey and some of the sweeter wines—glucose, it's called—that after a while, and in certain conditions, it *neutralizes potassium cyanide*. It can take an hour or two, depending on temperature, but eventually it eradicates the poison's most harmful properties. I could tell you more, but I doubt you'd understand it. Anyway, it's called the Kilini Reaction."

"I think I get it," said Mme. Petitquartier. "So the honey canceled out the poison?"

"If you like," her husband answered somewhat condescendingly. "Now, it was a honey tartlet, yes? And I was running late this morning—after all, you thought I'd already gone, didn't you? On my way out through the kitchen, I saw the tartlet. I was in a hurry, so I stuffed it into my pocket. I didn't have a chance to eat it until noon. Lucky me! By noon, the heat and the glucose had accelerated the reaction. But if I'd eaten it *at the time* it would have been a very different story indeed...."

The spindly spider-lover had (for the moment at least) gone up considerably in his wife's estimation. Like the shock, though, it would soon wear off.

Léon didn't breathe a word. He just sat there, stupefied, examining the vial of poison at arm's length. It seemed to hover before him in a thick fog.

"Come to bed, Paul," the pastry chef instructed.

# THE SALVATION OF MAXIM ZAPYROV

"It wasn't what you're thinking. It wasn't the eyes or the face. It was the fist. Like a great black block rolling slowly from side to side on the tabletop. Never still. Picture it. Each time the back of the hand touched the surface, I glimpsed a little of the palm, as though the hand were a blooming flower. Nails, old man, like rose petals. I couldn't take my eyes off that fist. My head was moving back and forth, to the rhythm of that rolling fist. Do you know what I mean? Of course you don't. You can't understand. It all happens here... and here..." he tapped his chest, then the side of his skull. "That's the way it is, old man."

He spat, and the sawdust on the floor slowly soaked up the saliva. He had high cheekbones and a face that was fuzzy with a week's worth of beard. The Métro, a bench, a porch, a construction site: each of these had been his bed over the past seven nights. His only food had come from garbage cans.

He drank, and for a moment or two he was lost in thought. Then, suddenly, his face seemed lit from within. It was as if he had glimpsed something through the haze of smoke and the stench of vinasse, an ineffable vision between the chipped ceiling and the murky walls. But this flame fluttered out as quickly as it had appeared. The man frowned and closed his eyes.

"What were you thinking about?"

"I... I was thinking about vodka, old man. And the snow. The snow in the Urals... But if you've never seen it, you won't understand."

"Landlord! Vodka!" shouted the man's companion.

"We've run out, M. Paul," said the landlord. "Can I get you calva instead?"

"No," said Paul, "we want vodka."

They were already fairly drunk. They left the bar and headed along a winding dark alley out onto the shiny cobblestones of place Maubert. It was one in the morning. The air was damp with drizzle.

"Hey!" said M. Paul. "I know a place."

They made their way up toward the Panthéon.

The fellow who had spoken nostalgically of snow in the Urals was named Maxim Zapyrov. A big man of some thirty years, he was the sort of Russian you read about in novels. Blond mane, cold eyes, pale skin. Unpredictable mood swings. A lust for life tempered by the inevitability of death. A man of infinite scruples, but incapable of what Westerners would call "modesty." Capable of the most absurd heroism and the most abject cowardice. A hero crippled by pride. Nostalgia for pure snow, but an instinct for the dirty Paris streets. He had no interest in philosophy, and yet he was acutely preoccupied with the infinite: death, the immortal soul, conscience, good, evil, God.... And above all, vodka. That was Maxim Zapyrov. He had arrived in Paris a week earlier with a hundred francs in his pocket and a French vocabulary of some fifty words. His first stop had been Montparnasse, to find succor at the bottom of a vodka glass.

*Sell that coat of yours,* the vodka had told him. *Sell your suitcase, too, and your spare linen. Then come back to me.*

So Zapyrov sold everything. Two hundred francs richer, he returned to consult the vodka once again. By dawn, he had no money at all. After some forty-eight hours of fasting, he had tried his hand at begging. But he didn't know how. Then he had embarked on the odious adventure which he was now attempting to recount to M. Paul—peppered with metaphysical asides.

A fine fellow, this M. Paul. Maxim had met him around midnight, in the bar near place Maubert. The bar which had now run out of vodka, but which never seemed to run out of beer, wine, or terrifying grain alcohols.

M. Paul was French. A pale old man, whose soft, sickly skin was the color of wilted lettuce. He had a flat face with ill-defined features, a shapeless mouth—like a hole scooped out of a mound of jelly. Glassy eyes, like a fish. A waste of space. But, for the moment at least, a *worthy* waste of space. For M. Paul had fifty francs in his pocket. And he spoke German—a language that Zapyrov, who did not know French, spoke fluently. So M. Paul was an ideal companion for the Russian. The two men ascended toward the Panthéon. They were going to find some vodka.

"Even worse," Zapyrov continued, "I had lost my glasses. Very unfortunate for a short-sighted fellow like me. Objects, people— I could only see them through a haze. And don't forget that I was starving. Starvation clouds a man's vision. So I couldn't really make out the features of the man sitting less than two meters from me. I can tell you that he was black, and that he was huge. I had not managed to catch him spying on me, and yet all the same I couldn't help but think that he was rolling his fist back and forth for me. All I could think about was that fist. I couldn't see anything else. To my poor eyes, he seemed to grow in stature, and become monstrous, like something from a nightmare. And I was terrified because I didn't want to imagine what would happen the moment that fist stopped moving."

They were halfway there. M. Paul stopped to catch his breath. "I don't understand," he said, "what..."

The Russian spoke confidentially. "Listen, old man, who are you? I've no idea. And yet I trust you. There's a voice in my head that tells me you're a good sort."

"No, no!" M. Paul protested. "I'm not good."

"Yes you are! And so am I; I'm good. Man is good, that's the general rule. But he finds it hard to admit, so he persuades himself that he's bad. That's the root of all evil. Am I right?"

"Perhaps," agreed M. Paul.

"Well, old man, I'd better tell you that I had good reason to fear a trap. Unfortunately, I still have reason. But because I don't know what the man who's after me looks like, I have to be very careful. All I can tell you is that he's black. You see, old man, I have blood on my hands. My conscience won't let me rest, I keep hearing the same word again and again—a word I can never repeat. And why? Because one night, in a street I would like to forget, there was a man stumbling from weariness and weeping with hunger, desperate and begging. What detestable thing happened in that dark and narrow street, I can never tell. Not even to you, my friend. All you need to know is that the next day the name of that street was all over the French newspapers. I tried to read the article, but couldn't decipher it. The only detail I understood was that a detective—*le détective noir*—was hunting for the beggar. And you guessed it—I was the beggar."

M. Paul raised a finger to his lips. "Shut your mouth. I don't want to know. Everyone has their secrets."

But Zapyrov continued: "I was the beggar... and a policeman was looking for me. A black policeman, that's all I know. Did you know the Sûreté hired black men?"

"Can't say I did," said M. Paul, "but it doesn't surprise me."

The Russian went on: "You may as well hear the rest of it,

old man. *Maxim Zapyrov,* I said to myself in the café, *that fellow over there rolling his fist back and forth is the man who's after you. It has to be him. He's found you. He's playing with you like a cat plays with a mouse. When he stops rolling his fist...* I waited. And, in the end, the fist stopped. The man got up, came and sat down beside me, placed his closed fist on the table, and looked at me. I tried my best to remain calm, but it wasn't easy I can tell you. Then he smiled, winked at me, and nodded toward the fist. I looked down, the fingers unclasped, and do you know what I saw? A watch! A gold watch, which must have been worth a pretty penny! The man closed his fingers round it again. 'Forty francs,' he said."

"So the man was a thief," said M. Paul.

"A thief!" repeated Zapyrov with a boisterous laugh. "The 'policeman' was a thief all along! Come on. Let's get some vodka."

Soon they were at the foot of the Panthéon. The Russian pointed towards it: "Tell me, do you believe God is in that church?"

"It's a mausoleum," said M. Paul in learned tones.

The other man reflected, then shrugged: "What does it matter? God is everywhere. That's what I believe. What about you? Do you believe in God? Be honest, now."

"I don't know," said M. Paul.

Zapyrov pounded his chest: "God exists! He is in me, like a disease. When I think of Him, my heart breaks, my organs melt." He was seized by a kind of fervor. He reached out and touched M. Paul's pale cheek with undeniable gentleness. "I love you, old man. I would like you to hear my confession. I would like to humble myself before you. But my tongue turns to ice as soon as I come to pronounce the word. A word that I can never repeat. Old man, I am a wastrel. A despicable creature, unworthy to walk by your side. You are a saint. Forgive me my sins. Absolve me."

"All right," said M. Paul uncomfortably. "I absolve you."

Zapyrov was crying, just like a Russian from a novel. He wanted to kiss M. Paul. He said: "I'm sad. It's good, this sadness. Humiliation is also good. Please, come. Let's get some vodka. We'd better hurry. Maybe the place is already closed. Yes, I think it's closed. Where else can we go?"

The bar was not in fact closed. Vodka wasn't particularly

popular there, so the owner sold it cheap. They drank several small glasses of the stuff. Zapyrov was silent.

Then, they were in the street once more. Two a.m. The drizzle had turned to stinging rain. M. Paul shivered and turned up the collar of his raincoat.

Zapyrov had no raincoat, but he was not cold. The miracle of vodka. He resumed his story where he had left off: "Once I knew the fellow wasn't a policeman but just another thief, I left the café and walked for a long time. Streets, alleys, squares. Sometimes I would pause in a square where children were playing, watched over by their mothers. The sight of them softened me somewhat, but it made me sadder, too. *Maxim Zapyrov,* I thought, *why aren't you as pure as those little creatures?* I despised myself, because I knew that my soul was wretched, and the feeling of abjection overwhelmed me. A terrible voice kept repeating the word that I dare not say. But I was confused, and torn. Beneath the sound of that terrible voice was another voice, a small voice, but just as stubborn as the first. *No, Maxim Zapyrov,* it said, *your soul is not wretched. You do not corrupt these little ones by your presence. You are worthy of them. You are as pure as the purest innocent!* I didn't know what to think. I looked to the sky for answers, but the only thing I felt was a dreadful cold. Old man, it was dreadful. I choked back my tears and carried on walking. I went straight ahead. I didn't even stop to notice the street names. What difference did it make? This great city, which had so excited my imagination when I was home in the distant Urals... Now I was here, and misfortune had found me. Among all those thousands of houses, there was not one in which I could lay my head and sleep."

Rue Soufflot. Rue de Medici. Rue de Vaugirard. Maxim Zapyrov and M. Paul walked. Rue Bonaparte. The docks of the Seine. For a few moments, the Russian let his gaze wander over the surface of the river. The water was deep and dark. He said: "I came upon a place larger than anything I had ever seen. In the center was an arch surrounded by chains-" (L'Arc de Triomphe, thought M. Paul) "—then I was in a kind of forest—" (Le Bois, thought M. Paul) "—paths threaded between the trees. I followed one. There were very few people around. Just a walker here and there, or a courting couple. Soon I lost myself in the foliage. I reached a place in the shadow of a number of saplings. There was a bench. I sat. I breathed freely in the cool air as dusk began to fall. It soothed me. I began to regain a sense of hope."

"When, behind a clump of nearby trees, I heard the crunch of twigs underfoot. Whispers. I approached, and saw the shape of two men lying side by side in the grass. Terror seized me immediately. Now I know what you're going to say, old man—how could I be sure these two men were after *me*, that one of them was the famous black detective? Surely it was a one in a million chance, I must be crazy!

"But listen: no sooner had those two men spotted me than they were on their feet, moving furtively away. Now, I ask you, why did they run? What were they doing, lying side by side in the grass? What *could* they be doing?

"I remained motionless for a moment. Stunned. Then I heard one of them laugh, and the sound filled me with indescribable horror. I needed to get back to the city. I needed busy streets, I needed to lose myself in the heart of a crowd.

"Night had come. I wandered under the street lamps—those globes of suspended flame. I saw many women walking those streets, made-up and perfumed. Some were very beautiful. I watched them with the same fascination that I would have watched the Blessed Virgin Herself. But with my sunken eyes, my messy beard, I disgusted them. They ignored me. There was not one among them—not *one*, do you hear?—who gave me so much as a pitying look. I tell you, old man, there is no pity in this world."

Quai Saint-Michel. Quai de Montebello. Quai de la Tournelle. Maxim Zapyrov and M. Paul crossed the Pont de Sully and passed into the City. They moved slowly, stopping frequently. Quai d'Anjou... Quai de Bourbon...

"Suddenly: horror! In one of those lamp-lit streets, I felt a hand on my shoulder.

"I turned. The man wore a uniform. He was black, of course. He said something in French; something I couldn't quite grasp. But the meaning was obvious: I was to follow him. The game was up. I obeyed.

"But guess what, old man! The game was not up, after all! The man led me to a luxury saloon car. He pointed to a large trunk on the roof. I understood at once that he was asking for my help in moving this burden. Imagine my elation! So not only did I help to unload the luggage, I also helped haul it up to the third floor of a nearby house: a wealthy place with a carpeted staircase. Then we entered an apartment which I could tell—even with just a cursory glance—was elegant and filled with treasures. I followed the man into a large, bright kitchen where two men and four women were standing around. I was no longer afraid; it was obvious these people were servants. One of them offered me some wine, which was excellent. I gave a laugh, to show my enjoyment. And now you must believe me when I tell you what happened next—before sending me on my way, they gave me the rest of the bottle! No word of a lie! As I walked back down the stairs I thought *Learn from this, Maxim Zapyrov! Learn! Love and charity* do *exist!* I was very hungry, but I decided to save what money I had for drinking. I walked for a long time, as fast as I could, looking to quench my thirst. The thought of sitting comfortably in a warm room and raising a glass to my lips was enough to keep me going.

"I had almost forgotten my fear. Almost forgotten my twilit adventure when, for the first time in my life, I begged. Such a vile and depraved experience. Finally, in a side street, I entered an establishment which I first took to be a cabaret. And while the booze was flowing freely, it was actually a dance hall. Imagine my horror, old man, when the fellow who served me vodka was a Negro. I dared not move. There was an orchestra: all Negroes. And the place was filled almost exclusively with a black clientele—" (the Bal Blomet, thought M. Paul) "—I was no longer afraid. There were simply too many for me to assume that one was the man out to get me. So I stayed awhile. I watched the couples dance. I even managed to enjoy myself a little. How was I to know what was about to happen? Soon, all those whirling bodies made me dizzy. You must remember that I had lost my glasses, so my vision was blurred. And don't forget I had not eaten for a long time, either. I felt as though my head were spinning round and round on my neck like a top. I began to hallucinate. I saw that all the men in that dance hall were in fact just one man, duplicated infinitely. *Le detective noir.* The man who was after me.

He was dancing and contorting himself in all corners of the hall. He had fifty mouths, all talking at once. He was on stage, playing ten instruments at the same time. He had a napkin over his arm, serving liquor at twenty different tables, which he immediately drank from forty glasses. But don't think that for one second he took his eyes off me! It was him! The black

detective. My soul was filled with dread once again. I was sweat-
ing, my teeth chattered. I thought I might collapse. I pleaded
with God to show mercy, to give me the energy to move. Soon
enough the paralysis lifted, I was able to get out of there. And
then, not two hours after that little adventure, I ran into you,
and we began our conversation. So now you know everything,
old man."

Pont Saint Louis. Quai aux Fleurs. Quai de l'Horloge. Maxim
Zapyrov was silent. On the bridge, the two men paused. Leaning
over the parapet, they contemplated the swirls of black water,
speckled with foam.

"That's what happened," muttered the Russian. "He was
everywhere, swirling round me like a whirlwind..."

Thereupon, a fairly long silence descended. And suddenly,
with a ferocity as violent as it was abrupt: "Dog!" exclaimed
Maxim Zapyrov. "Dog that I am! I wanted you to absolve me,
old man, but I have not confessed my sin. Now listen..."

"Be quiet," said M. Paul gently.

"I will not be quiet! I must not! I cannot! My sin burns
inside me. It moves and thrashes, like a child waiting to burst
from the womb. Listen to me. I killed a man. You have been
drinking with a murderer."

M. Paul sighed weakly.

"It was on that fateful night I told you about. The name of
the street is rue de l'Abbé-de-l'Épée. Since dawn, I had been
in utter despair. There was a demon at my shoulder, walking
beside me all day long, telling me to end it all. Suddenly there
was a man. A rich man, with a fur-lined overcoat, bowler hat,
gaiters on his shoes, and a gold-tipped cane. He was coming
towards me. I was hungry. I prostrated myself, pleading for alms.
He passed by without a word. So I followed him, like a dog, still
begging. I was so hungry! Soon enough, he stopped and began
to curse at me. I did not move. His face flushed, his voice grew
louder. I realized he was threatening me. But I continued to
beg, holding out my hand. He hit me with his cane. That was
when I thought, old man, *There is no pity in this world*. None.
Rage coursed through me, I reached up and grabbed him by
the throat and... Weak as I was, how did it happen? Between my
fingers, his neck cracked. He dropped instantly to the pavement.
I couldn't believe my eyes. I swear on my immortal soul, I did

not mean to kill him. And yet the man was dead. And a voice at my shoulder whispered *Murderer*....

"I turned around: there was no one there. I did not search the dead man's pockets for money. I ran. But everywhere I went, the voice pursued me: *Murderer... Murderer...* Later, I realized I had lost my glasses. Probably in the struggle. I passed by the police station and thought about giving myself up. But I didn't have the courage. Then I went to the river, planning to end it all. But again I failed. Because I'm a coward. Maxim Zapyrov is a coward. Since then I have just been wandering, pursued by this 'detective noir' the papers talked about. I don't know much French, but I do know that. So what do I do? I just want to lie down. Is that so much to ask? I don't even want a bed. Not even a carpet. A bare stone floor would be enough. I just need a good night's rest. I want the chase to be over. I want to sleep."

"Come with me," said M. Paul. "I know a place."

They took the quai des Orfèvres. M. Paul reached into his pocket for something. "Zapyrov," he asked, "these are your glasses, aren't they?"

The Russian recognized them instantly. M. Paul looked at him sadly. "Zapyrov," he went on, "chance is a funny thing. Of all the people in this city, you fell right into the hands of the very man who was looking for you. Your French is not as bad as you think, but it's not good enough. You misread 'detective noir' in the newspaper. I am the detective. My name is Paul Noir."

Zapyrov considered his companion for a long time. "Chance?" he said finally, in a dull voice. "Chance? Or fate?" He added: "I'm glad it's you. Because you are a good man."

"I'm neither good nor bad," said the other. "I'm *le detective Noir*."

They advanced. The inspector was pensive. Zapyrov was breathing heavily.

"I'm angry, Zapyrov," said Paul Noir. "If I'd simply caught you, I would have arrested you without hesitation. But now that I've got to know you, now that I've heard your story..."

He reached a decision. Through the curtain of rain, he gestured at the deserted streets.

"Listen. We didn't drink together. You didn't say a word to me. I don't know you. Go away."

Zapyrov flinched.

On the right was the Seine. On his left, *la Tour Pointue*.

Alternatively, the Russian gazed between the river and the building's dark façade. His face reflected a deep inner conflict. The policeman was waiting. And, little by little, he saw the Russian's tense expression relax. An almost joyous look replaced the profound anguish. Finally, an air of relief transformed the ravaged face. Maxim Zapyrov stammered out a few words— *Redemption...Atonement...*—then, shaking his head, he held out his wrists for the handcuffs.

"Let's go," he said.

# THE SPANISH PRISONER

M. Celestin Lainé,
Argenteuil,
France.

Dear sir,
I am currently in prison for bankruptcy and I am compelled to ask if you would be willing to help me retrieve the sum of one million eight hundred thousand francs from a trunk which is held in a French railway station. This would require you to pay for my belongings (including the receipt for the trunk) to be released. You will need this in order to collect said trunk from the station.

By way of reward, I will give you one third of the cash contained in the trunk. I am unable to receive correspondence in prison, but if you wish to accept my offer, please send a telegram via a trusted third party, who will pass the message on to me. In case this letter does not reach you, I shall await your reply before revealing my name. Thus, I sign:
C.
Please send telegram as follows: Ricardo y Mendez, Pablo Correos, 117. Sevilla. Spain: Message received, Lainé.
Do not reply.

*

Having read this singular missive aloud, Jussiot burst out laughing and thumped his friend Celestin Lainé on the shoulder. This caused Lainé—a somewhat puny individual with a head the size of a fist—to sink about six inches into his seat at the Café des Quatre Ancres.

"Only one million eight hundred thousand? Not even the full two million? Peanuts! He's a modest fellow, this 'prisoner' of yours! What do you reckon, Madame Eveline?"

"I reckon," replied Madame Eveline, "that the 'Spanish prisoner' trick is a bit old-hat."

With that, she finished her Pernod in one gulp and ordered another with an imperious flick of her index finger—a superfluous gesture, for Philippe the waiter was already dashing over, bottle in hand.

The clock chimed half-past eleven. With it came an explosion of yelling from the back room: a distinguished-looking belote player was peppering his opponent with insults, the latter fellow having missed a "call." This onslaught would have caused a brawl in any other circumstances. But the man in question remained calm, knowing full well that belote without insults is scarcely belote at all.

M. Lormoise protested, "I disagree, Madame Eveline. Just because a trick is old doesn't mean it ceases to work. Far from it! The Spanish prisoner has been around for over a century. In another century, I'm sure it will still be going strong. It's as reliable as human stupidity."

M. Moutier shared Lormoise's opinion. He cited the case of a merchant from Toulouse who had traveled to the far side of the Pyrenees some six months ago, taking with him a handsome amount of money, and had not been seen since. "What puzzles me," he continued, "and I mean no offence, Lainé, but why should they target you of all people?"

Lainé was hardly an appealing prospect for a confidence trickster. He did not have a penny to his name. He went about his job as a door-to-door salesman with more zeal than success, and barely scraped enough money to cover his travel expenses, his tobacco, and his drink.

Fortunately, this pitiful character had five friends, all very rich and respectable: Urbain Moutier, owner of the Café des Quatre Ancres, Quai de Montebello, Paris. Camille Jussiot, retired baker; Léon-Paul Touzerie, draper, Lucas Lormoise, bookmaker; finally, Madame Eveline Lafraie, sculptress, whose works were very fashionable in America.

Lainé did odd jobs for them all. For Madame Eveline, for instance, he was an occasional model. And in recognition of services rendered (but really out of pity) the five of them clubbed together to provide the poor devil with five hundred francs a month—just enough for him to get by. And between ten and midnight every evening they met for drinks at the Café des Quatre Ancres.

It was during one of these get-togethers that Lainé had caused a sensation by producing a letter from this decidedly uninspired

"Spanish prisoner." As Lormoise was quick to observe, "Why Lainé? Might as well try and get blood out of a stone."

"They will have found my name in the *Bottin Mondain*," Celestin speculated.

"In the *Mondain*? You're not in the *Mondain*, are you?"

"But of course!"

This was true—at the beginning of the year, Lainé had come up with the bright idea of listing himself in the *Bottin Mondain* with not one but two addresses: the Café des Quatre Ancres, and a "summer retreat" in Argenteuil. The latter was a tiny but well-furnished place (worth between twenty and thirty thousand francs) which he had inherited.

He explained to his stunned benefactors, "The listing set me back forty francs, but it could be useful from a business perspective."

"Well, it seems to be working," retorted Lormoise. "Six hundred grand already! When are you leaving for Seville?"

Lainé smiled sadly. The last trip he had taken *anywhere* was an expenses-paid excursion to Moumelon-le-Petit, near Chalons, where he had been cordially invited to complete his military service. "I'd love to go to Spain," he sighed. "I hear it's beautiful. Alas, not this year."

The conversation shifted to the potential consequences of a positive reply to the Spanish prisoner.

"I suppose they would arrange a meeting," said Madame Eveline, "to which you would be expected to bring a large sum of money. Enough to retrieve this famous luggage receipt. Then they would rob you, strip you, and leave you naked in a ditch somewhere."

"If he's lucky," Moutier added. "They might simply slit his throat to keep him quiet."

Lainé brought this discussion to an unexpected conclusion: he offered to settle the bill.

"Spending your six hundred thousand already?"

Lainé produced three hundred francs from his pocket. Thanks to a tip "borrowed" from one of his colleagues, he'd been able to assist a young couple who then rewarded him handsomely.

Their drinks were refreshed.

"To your health, little man!" Mme Eveline shouted at Lainé, gulping down her fourth Pernod of the evening.

The clock struck a quarter past twelve. Lainé jumped. "If I want to catch my connection at Réaumur, I'd better be off...."

But Madame Eveline stopped him. "Just a moment, little man! I need you to pose for me at the studio tomorrow. I have an idea for a tableau: Job sur son manure. Will you come?"

"Naturally," said Lainé, "you would like me to be Job?"

"Of course. Does that bother you?"

"Oh, you know me. Job or Croesus, I don't mind."

"Hey," put in Jussiot, "today Job, tomorrow Croesus! Six hundred grand is not to be sniffed at, Celestin."

Deathly afraid of missing his connection, Celestin Lainé, also known as "little man," dashed out without another word, and made for the Saint-Michel métro at an ungainly trot.

But as he walked, he murmured to himself, "Six hundred thousand! If only it were true..."

Back at Moutier's café, an idea was germinating in Jussiot's mind. A final shot of alcohol brought it to life. "Here's a thought. What if, without telling the little man, we were to telegram *message received* to the Spanish prisoner as instructed? Then Celestin would be able to show us the reply. An amusing notion, don't you agree?"

By four votes to one (Lormoise remained cautious) they agreed to the scheme.

The next morning, Moutier sent the telegram.

Three days went by. Then four. Then a week...

As usual, Lainé continued to make himself useful by posing as Job at Mme Eveline's studio.

Occasionally one or another of the accomplices would raise the subject of the Spanish prisoner, just to gauge the little man's reaction.

"Not still dwelling on that stupid scheme, are you?" said Lainé.

It was obvious he had received no further communication. Apparently Seville had become too dangerous for Señor Ricardo y Mendez, who must have decamped without leaving a forwarding address.

But then, on the tenth day, something happened.

"Who's that?" Moutier asked his waiter, Philippe, nodding toward an unfamiliar customer: a swarthy fellow with eccentric dress sense who was practicing billiards by himself.

Philippe did not know him. "All I can tell you is, he has a

foreign accent. Italian, I'd say. And look at the way he plays! Ridiculous! I'll bet you he's going to damage the table."

Philippe's indignation was justified. Not only was this fellow hopeless at billiards, he did not even seem to be paying attention.

Moutier could not stand it for long. He approached the stranger and spoke diplomatically. "Excuse me, sir... No offence, but this is a match billiard table, you understand. It's designed for players of a certain class and don't you think... wouldn't it be best..." He grew suddenly impatient. "Don't you think you've played enough?"

The other man listened intently, nodded, and flashed his teeth in a broad grin. But as soon as Moutier had finished, he returned to the table with more determination than ever. He had not understood a single word.

Furious, Moutier got between him and the table, yelling, "I told you I was sick of you messing about with my billiard table! If you can't speak French, why don't you go back to your own country?"

Far from being irritated, the stranger put down his cue, smiled even more broadly, and replied with a strong accent, "My country: Spain. Very beautiful country. You visit?" He caressed the edge of the billiard table affectionately. "I play a little. Not so much."

Then he went to sit down and ordered booze and a deck of cards.

He sat for an hour or so, doing card tricks. He looked up each time the door opened, scrutinizing the new arrivals.

"He's waiting for someone," observed Philippe.

Soon after, and without any notable incident, the Spaniard settled his bill, saluted politely, and left.

It was only later that evening, when Jussiot, Touzerie and Lormoise appeared, that Moutier grew suspicious. "That foreigner... the Spaniard... suppose he was something to do with the Spanish-prisoner gang? Suppose he came because of the telegram?"

He shared his concern with his three friends. With comically exaggerated concern, the bookmaker pressed his palm to Moutier's forehead. "Hey, you're burning up!" He turned to Jussiot, "What do you think?"

"I think he needs a drink," replied a chuckling Jussiot. "Philippe—bring us a bottle! And four glasses!"

"But if you'd seen this fellow..." Moutier persisted.

"Look out!" Lormoise interrupted.

But it was only Madame Eveline and Celestin Lainé, entering the café arm in arm.

A quarter of an hour later, Moutier gave Jussiot, Touzerie and Lormoise a discreet wink. The Spaniard had just reappeared.

They studied him with interest.

"What is it?" asked Madame Eveline, nursing her Pernod.

They did not answer her.

Smiling widely at Moutier, the stranger then went over to the bar and ordered a coffee.

Madame Eveline then began to speak excitedly about her work in progress: *Job sur son manure*. She ruffled Celestin's mop of hair. "Amazing! Gorgeous!" she enthused. "You must all come and see it next week. Lainé is perfect for Job. He really looks like a starving man. We're going to create a masterpiece, aren't we, my darling Lainé?"

Moutier, Jussiot, Touzerie and Lormoise noticed the stranger glance in their direction. His gaze rested briefly on Celestin Lainé's face, then flicked away.

This disturbed the four men.

Five minutes later, the Spaniard paid his bill, straightened his tie in the mirror, grinned at Moutier once more, and left.

"Madame Eveline," the bookmaker muttered, "do you have to talk so loud? 'Lainé this, Lainé that...' We know his name is Lainé!"

"What's the matter?" Celestin wondered aloud.

Madame Eveline shrugged. "Let them grumble, little man! They are philistines, incapable of enthusiasm. But you and I, my Job, are artists!"

*

The next morning, as Celestin Lainé was leaving the Café des Quatre Ancres, a man came up to him with a question. Moutier sprang from behind his counter. He had recognized the Spaniard.

"Place de l'hotel-de-ville?" he heard Lainé repeat. "I'm heading that way myself. Perhaps I'd better show you."

The two men walked away. Somewhat disturbed, Moutier followed—but there was no need. When they reached the place de l'hotel-de-ville, the Spaniard thanked Lainé effusively and disappeared into the Bazaar.

"I don't like this. I don't like this at all," Moutier grumbled to himself as he headed back.

At the earliest possible moment, he notified his three friends and Madame Eveline.

"I think we may have made a mistake in sending that telegram," Lormoise commented after some thought. "Perhaps we ought to call the police?"

"Police? Oh, very funny," replied the bookmaker.

"We should at least tell Lainé what's going on. Can't be too careful."

So, that evening, they did.

"Very droll, I'm sure!" Lainé exclaimed. But he was not unduly concerned, and told them the Spaniard had not behaved suspiciously toward him. And besides, he added, Lormoise was right: this gang of criminals might as well try and draw blood from a stone.

Four days went by.

Lainé continued to pose for Madame Eveline. The sketches for *Job sur son manure* progressed briskly.

The Spaniard did not reappear.

"A lot of fuss about nothing," Touzerie concluded with satisfaction.

"I wonder," said Madame Eveline thoughtfully. "There's something the matter with the little man. I see him every day, so I have had the opportunity to study him. Since his meeting with the Spaniard, and what we told him about the telegram, he's changed. Can't you see that all this talk of six hundred thousand francs is getting to him?"

"Of course not! He's not stupid."

But the following day, Madame Eveline's assessment was proven correct. While waiting for a train at the Sèvres–Babylone métro station, Lormoise saw Lainé and the Spaniard together on the opposite platform. They were engaged in animated conversation. The Spaniard was showing some papers to Lainé.

The bookmaker tried to attract the little man's attention, but before he managed it both trains arrived in the station together.

That evening, Celestin did not appear at the Quatre Ancres.

"Obviously he's been shanghaied by the Spaniard," said Madame Eveline.

Partly from worry and partly because the group felt directly responsible—after all, nothing would have happened if not for their absurd telegram—it was decided that a reliable fellow, one of the bookmaker's men, would follow Lainé for a few days. He'd be there in case any difficulties should arise.

Unfortunately, this did not last long.

In one of the narrow, badly lit, and generally deserted streets which adjoin the quais, Lormoise's emissary pursued Lainé at a brisk pace. He did not once suspect that he himself might also be under surveillance. Which turned out to be the case. Without realizing what was happening, he received a swift blow to the back of the head with a sandbag, which knocked him out for the count.

When he came to, the street was deserted.

Sheepishly, he did the only thing he could think of: he headed back to Les Quatre Ancres to make his report.

The next morning, there was no sign of Lainé.

He did not appear in the afternoon either, when he was expected at Madame Eveline's studio. And Lainé was punctuality personified.

That evening, there was no Lainé.

Over the next two days, there was no sign at all. What had happened to him?

"It would make sense if he had any money—I'd guess that they'd robbed him. But all the little man has going for him is his looks!"

"But he could have convinced the Spaniard that he had money."

They needed to act quickly.

Piling into Moutier's car, they drove to Argenteuil.

Outside the Lainé place, they stopped. The shutters and doors were locked. The place was deserted.

A neighbor furnished them with some disturbing information: the previous day, M. Lainé—accompanied by a strange-looking foreigner—had piled all his furniture into a van.

"You see! The fool has got his heart set on that six hundred thousand. He sold his furniture to pay for that suitcase and the famous luggage receipt. He'll be back in a day or two with his tail between his legs..."

*

But Lainé did not return.

Eight days went by, then ten... At the Quatre Ancres there was a pervasive atmosphere of anxiety mingled with remorse. They came up with various plans of action, but none of them held up under scrutiny. Call the police? Apart from the fact that an official inquiry would have been almost certainly futile, the bookmaker was filled with mortal horror at the mere thought of entering a police station. As well as this, the others did not much care for the notion of the ridicule that would inevitably be heaped on them when the story got out. They were supposed to be professionals, every one of them. And what an advertisement this would be for Madame Eveline's artwork!

So they waited.

And waited.

Two weeks... Three weeks...

And the end of the third week, news arrived in the form of a letter from Lainé. It had come from Seville.

Written in pencil in a shaking hand, it read:

*I am a prisoner of the Spanish prisoner. He has me locked up in a cellar in a place called Triana.*

Then came a moving passage:

*I was a fool! The thought of the six hundred thousand francs drove me mad. I was so tired of being poor. Try to understand... I sold my furniture to come here, and they robbed me. But it wasn't my money they were after: it was yours! They know I have wealthy friends, and they say that if you don't pay a ransom of forty-thousand francs they'll starve me to death and throw me in the Guadalquivir—that's a river here. Please help me, save me! If you help me, when I get back to Argenteuil I will sell my house and you can have the proceeds. Then I'll work for you for free until the rest of the debt is paid off. But please, for God's sake, have pity on this "little man."*

*If you are willing, please publish an ad in one of the major Paris newspapers. They have accomplices there. On the specified day and time, an emissary will come into Les Quatre Ancres and you will hand over the cash in banknotes. If you say a word to the police, or try to intercept this emissary in any way, then I will die.*

*Your unfortunate,*

*Lainé*

In Moutier's apartment above Les Quatre Ancres, a fierce debate raged long into the night. Although each member of that group was a millionaire, the prospect of paying forty thousand francs—eight thousand per person—to a criminal gang did not appeal to any of them.

But in the end, friendship and guilt triumphed over self-interest. Madame Eveline also pointed out that the sale of the place at Argenteuil would cover half the sum.

Therefore, it was decided between them that they would go along with the kidnappers' instructions. The next day, they had the announcement printed in the paper and, two days later, the sinister-looking fellow they had previously seen around the place returned to the Café des Quatre Ancres. Moutier led him through to the kitchen and, while the others watched, handed him the forty thousand francs.

The man counted the money, then growled, "Very well. Your friend will be returned to you tomorrow."

He then left the bar without haste.

A quarter of an hour later, the telephone rang. The caller asked for Madame Eveline.

"Hello? Yes, Madame Eveline here. Who's this? Who? Little man? Celestin, it's you!"

"Yes, it's really me, my dear friend. And no, I am not calling from the depths of a cellar in Seville, but from a train station in Paris. I just wanted to tell you that the Spanish prisoner trick may well be 'old hat' but it is certainly not without its merits, as my demonstration proves!

"It was very simple. The first letter, the one I showed you, was genuine. When I received the second, I guessed that you had played a hilarious joke by sending a telegram in my name. So, I decided to play you at your own game. I came up this scheme with the assistance of a friend of mine.

"As for Seville, my dear Eveline, if you should ever desire to send correspondence bearing the stamp of a country in which you have never set foot, I can recommend the Nenufar Agency. They have correspondents all over the globe.... Impeccable organization, reasonable prices, quick and discreet...

"One last thing: my place in Argenteuil... there's no need to bother putting it up for sale. I already did that three weeks ago.

"With that, I bid you adieu, Madame Eveline. Please pass my regards on to the others... not forgetting *Job sur son manure.*"

# THE 700,000 PINK RADISHES

"What's the matter?" demanded M. Gour.

It was Thursday, May 2nd—the Feast of St. Athanasius. Léopold Charpinel, secretary to the great Parisian publisher M. Hippolyte Gour, had just burst out laughing as he read through the morning correspondence.

He handed his boss a typed letter with the following letterhead:

*ARTHUR RIMBAUD AND SON*
*Fruit, Groceries, Seeds*
*27, rue du Souvenir, ROSCOFF (Finistère)*

The humor was not immediately apparent.

*M. Léopold Charpinel*
*Éditions du Vieux-Monde*
*54, rue Milton, Paris-IXe*

*Roscoff, April 30, 1935*

*Sir,*

*Following our recent telephone conversation, we are pleased to inform you that we now have the requested stock of 700,000 pink radishes. They are guaranteed fresh and free of worm bites.*

*In the event that your employer, M. Gour, does indeed wish to purchase all of this stock, we will be pleased to sell it to him at a rate of 1/2 centime per radish. Therefore the total cost will be: Frs 3500 (three thousand, five hundred francs).*

*Delivery will be made as normal, that is to say in boxes of one hundred kilos, to be picked up at Montparnasse station, postage paid by the recipient.*

*In anticipation of your notifying M. Gour of our offer, and in the hope of a prompt and positive response, please accept our most cordial good wishes.*

*Signed on behalf of Arthur Rimbaud:*
*His son, Jules Rimbaud*

*P.S. As is customary, your commission will be 700,000 radish leaves. These will be dispatched to your personal address.*

The envelope bore the postmark of the post office at 96, rue Glück.

Publishing magnate M. Gour was a slender, monocled man who did not so much smoke as chew huge cigars. "What is this foolishness...?" he began. At the same time, a large fellow burst into the office without knocking.

"Good morning, you old rascal," he said cordially. It was the famous novelist Georges Martin, a childhood friend of Gour.

"Good morning, you reprobate," Gour answered. "What are you doing here? And why can't you knock like everybody else?"

"I need money," Martin declared, sinking into an armchair. He earned plenty from his books, but had expensive tastes in women.

"Money!" Gour roared. "You just had a year's advance! You won't get a single radish, I promise you that." As soon as he had spoken this last sentence, both Gour and Charpinel laughed.

"What's the matter with you two?" asked an astonished Martin.

"Listen," said Gour, "I don't have any money for you, but I can get you a wonderful deal...." He held out the letter about the 700,000 pink radishes.

Martin read it, then replied laconically, "Very funny."

At that moment, there came a knock at the door. It was the sales manager.

"Boss, we've got to decide about the Grand Prix de l'Académie. We need to try and grow..."

"Radishes?" put in Martin. "No need. You have seven hundred thousand at your disposal, chum."

The sales manager was suffering badly with sciatica, and was in a terrible mood. He skimmed the letter, and grimaced: "This is funny to you? It doesn't take much to make you laugh, it seems."

Thereupon the head of production entered the office. He was a capable but somewhat insincere young man. He in turn read the greengrocer's missive and chuckled. "Oh, I see—it's a joke. May I?" He borrowed the note and took it to the upper floor to show the art director. "Take a look at this beauty from Arthur Rimbaud..."

Meanwhile, Georges Martin returned his attention to M. Gour. "Well? What about my money?"

"You won't stop till I'm bankrupt, will you?" Gour sighed, writing out a check.

Martin pouted. "Five thousand? How am I supposed to live on that? The least you could do is buy me lunch...."

"What more do you want from me? My daughter's hand in marriage?" growled M. Gour, who was unmarried. "Very well, you shall have it. Grab a cigar. I suppose you have a match?"

"Not a single match. All I have is my big mouth," the famous author declared, taking a cigar and leaning toward the lighter that Léopold Charpinel held out to him.

On Wednesday May 8th—the Feast of St. Désiré—Charpinel's trip to the mail room at *Éditions du Vieux-Monde* turned up a new letter from Arthur Rimbaud and Son.

*Roscoff, May 6, 1935.*

*Sir,*

*Following receipt of your letter of the fourth of this month we are pleased to inform you that we are now preparing the packaging and dispatch of 700,000 pink radishes to Montparnasse station in Paris.*

*However, we are obliged to inform you that we will not be able to proceed with the shipment until payment is received. Specifically: 3,500 francs.*

*Regarding your commission (radish leaves), we will send these by post as soon as we receive the check or money order from M. Gour.*

*Thank you for your assistance in this matter, and please accept our most cordial greetings.*

*Signed on behalf of Arthur Rimbaud:*
*His son, Jules Rimbaud*

*The envelope bore a stamp from the post office at 27, rue Amélie.*
*It goes without saying that Charpinel had no more placed an order with the bizarre Maison Rimbaud than he had spoken with them on the telephone.*
*This latest letter was met with shrugs from M. Gour and the sales manager, then made its way around the publishing house staff, finally ending up screwed into a ball in the bottom of a wastepaper basket.*

On Monday, May 13th—the Feast of St. Onesimus—Charpinel received a telegram.

*Acknowledge receipt of check. Preparing shipment of 700,000 radishes and sending your commission. Kind regards.*

*Jules Rimbaud.*

This telegram, sent from the post office at number 5, rue de l'Épée-de-Bois, provoked further hilarity.

Two days passed.

On the third day, at eight o'clock in the morning, Charpinel's landlady entered his apartment and found him unconscious in pajamas on the parquet floor of his bedroom. The air was filled with the stench of chloroform. Beneath Charpinel's body was a bed of green radish leaves.

The secretary declared that he had been awoken at about half-past seven by the slamming of a door. Intrigued, he had got up, made a rapid inspection of the apartment. As he entered the bathroom, he had seen a kind of green ghost emerge from the bathtub; at the same time, somebody grabbed him from behind and placed a chloroform-soaked cloth over his mouth and nostrils.

Suddenly, the joke did not seem so funny.

Towards the end of the morning, Charpinel was seized by violent stomach pains and vomiting. His face took on a surprising yellowish tint. By nightfall, it covered his whole body. It was jaundice, brought on by shock. Charpinel was admitted to the hospital.

*

"Oh no, this is too much!" exclaimed Eugène de Pontarche, brandishing a letter.

"What is it?" asked M. Gour.

It was May 21st—the Feast of St. Hospitius. At Éditions du Vieux-Monde, *under-secretary Eugène de Pontar*che had temporarily stepped in to take over Charpinel's duties. And he had just now received a missive bearing the letterhead of the absurd greengrocers, Rimbaud and Sons. This letter was an exact duplicate of the first, which Charpinel had received on May 2nd.

*Following our recent telephone conversation, we are pleased to inform you that we now have the requested stock of 700,000 pink radishes...*

The only variation was the replacement of Charpinel's name with that of Eugène de Pontarche. He was also promised a commission in the form of radish leaves.

The envelope bore a postmark of the post office at number 83, rue Bleue.

Like the previous ones, this letter made the rounds of the publishing house. But no one was laughing now. They were now wondering what sort of plot was unfolding. The letter writer's goal remained a mystery, but there could be no doubt that it was something sinister.

And the business continued. On Saturday, May 25th—the Feast of St. Urbain—the next letter arrived:

*Following receipt of your letter of the twenty-third of this month we are pleased to inform you that we are now preparing the packaging and dispatch of 700,000 pink radishes...*

The envelope bore the postmark of the post office at number 121, rue des Fêtes.

Eugène de Pontarche was a timorous fellow, and did not hide his unease. He envisioned the inevitable arrival of grotesque greenery, the harbinger of a chloroform attack.

Somewhat concerned, but above all irritated, M. Gour called

in a private detective. The detective established without difficulty that there was no greengrocer in Roscoff by the name of
Rimbaud. Nor was there a rue du Souvenir. He examined every
typewriter in the publishing house, as well as those at the homes
of several employees and various printing works owned by M.
Gour. No result.

And on Saturday, June 1st—the Feast of St. Pamphilus—the
predicted telegram arrived, sent from the post office at number
40, rue Étienne-Dolet.

*Acknowledge receipt of check...*

Eugène de Pontarche no longer dared return home. He was
staying with a friend.

On the third day, passers-by witnessed a car draw up at the
curb outside the publishing house. Its door was thrown open
and Eugène de Pontarche was violently hauled into the vehicle,
which sped away and disappeared before the onlookers could
intervene. Luckily, one of them had the presence of mind to
write down the license number. The vehicle was found the next
day, abandoned in a field not far from Brunoy. It was stolen. On
the seats were found Eugène de Pontarche's hat, a rag soaked
in chloroform, a gag, and a few handfuls of radish leaves.

Police searched for eight days—all in vain. There was no
sign of Eugène de Pontarche, nor of his captor. As for Charpinel, his jaundice showed no sign of receding.

The immediate consequence of this preposterous affair was
that M. Gour found it impossible to hire a third secretary. There
were no viable candidates—everyone was terrified that they
would receive the two letters, the telegram, and the final leafy
assault.

The affair was so notorious that it attracted the attention
of a band of popular mystery novelists. There were three of
them. They had a professional interest in this intrigue, which
was easily as bewildering as those they came up with to fox
their readers. Following several conversations on café terraces,
they decided to invite the sales manager of *Éditions du Vieux-
Monde* out to lunch.

As soon as their guest sat down, they congratulated him.

"Your 'radishes' were a stroke of genius!"

"My radishes? I don't understand...."

"Now, now! We know a thing or two about mystery, you see. And we have solved this particular mystery. Now tell us, when does the book come out?"

"What book?"

"The Affair of the 700,000 Pink Radishes, of course!"

"Gentlemen, I assure you..."

"Calm yourself! Don't forget, we're in the business too! Now, just between us, who's the author?"

The three mystery writers had concluded that the letters, the attack on Charpinel, the kidnapping of Eugène de Pontarche, the chloroform, and the radish leaves were all part of an elaborate publicity stunt, carried out with the full knowledge of M. Gour and his two secretaries, to launch the debut novel of a brand-new author. But the sales manager was quick to set them straight.

"You are sure? But then..."

The three authors fell silent. One smoked a cigar, one a pipe, the other a cigarette. The cigar-smoker's main character was an exceptionally shrewd *juge de paix*; the pipe-smoker's was a remarkably sharp-witted policeman whose skill belied his apparent clumsiness; the cigarette-smoker's was a private detective whose subtle ways bordered on sorcery. These works had not made them rich, but they were comfortable—not to mention very confident in their talents and amiably condescending toward each other. The sales manager was somewhat amused to find these mystery specialists racking their brains to unravel the explanation of the Mystery of the 700,000 Pink Radishes.

They were trying to apply the methods of their fictional detectives. But what seems easy in fiction is much less so in real life....

After a period of laborious cogitations, one of them concluded, "So now we just have to wait for the damned radishes."

\*

The radishes arrived five days later, on Monday, June 17th—the Feast of Saint Avit....

It was the porter at *Éditions du Vieux-Monde* who found them. There were not quite 700,000; more like fifty, strung together in a rosary. The rosary was handing from the doorknob of the director's office.

They were magnificent radishes, perfectly ripe and free of worm bites, as promised in the letter signed by Jules Rimbaud. They had also been carefully stripped of their leaves.

They were examined by police and found to be perfectly untainted, and fit for consumption.

As to who had placed them there, it was impossible to tell.

*

On Tuesday June 18th—the Feast of St. Marine—M. Gour returned from lunch to find that a bouquet of roses which he had left on his desk had now disappeared. In its place was a bouquet of pink radishes, sewn together and stripped of their leaves.

M. Gour walked distractedly toward the window and rested his forehead against the glass. Lining the sidewalk all the way to the outskirts of Notre-Dame-de-Lorette was a parade of market sellers. One of them, just below the window, was selling bunches of pink radishes. Gour gave a start, then rushed out of his office. But he stopped short on the stairs.

*Am I going crazy? What does that old woman have to do with this?*

No sooner was he back in his office than someone knocked.

"Who's there?" the editor called out in a curiously strangled voice.

"It's me," said the head of production, poking his startled face round the door. "I wanted to ask you about the Prix Goncourt...."

"Later. I'm busy. Go away, please."

Gour hurled the radishes into a wastepaper basket and paced over to his bookshelves. There, he spotted something. One of the spines read:

*ARTHUR RIMBAUD*
*Complete Works*

Arthur Rimbaud... Rimbaud and Son... Roscoff, rue du Souvenir... Signed on behalf of Arthur Rimbaud: His son, Jules... Leaves... 3500 francs... Montparnasse station...

M. Gour smacked his desk.

The publishing house now boasted two new proof-readers: undercover policemen disguised as literary types. They were watching at all times. But even this was not enough to reassure the publisher.

Again there came a knock at M. Gour's door. It was the novelist, Georges Martin.

"Money, please," he moaned from the threshold. "I need money right away. It's life or death."

Seized by a cold fury, M. Gour rushed at him and threw him out. In the hallway he bumped into a postman, who handed him a registered parcel. Dispatched from the post office at number 77, rue de la Reine-Blanche, this parcel contained more leafless pink radishes.

On the landing, the editor noticed a young man seated in a corner. He approached him suspiciously. "Who are you? What are you doing here?"

"My name is Hector Gitan, sir," the man stammered. "I'm a novelist. I've brought you my first manuscript: The Vegetarian Vampire. It's a comedy."

"Oh really? Is that so?" demanded an exasperated M. Gour. "A comedy! *The Vegetarian Vampire*! And what does this vampire of yours eat? Pink radishes, I suppose?"

"I... don't know, sir...." the other answered quietly.

"Get the hell out of here!" Gour yelled. "Get out, and if I see you lurking round here again I swear I'll..."

This obsession with pink radishes had caused M. Gour to hallucinate. The painted fingernails of typists looked like radishes. Medals in soldiers' buttonholes looked like radishes. It was enough to drive him mad.

Eight days passed. There were no more letters, no more deliveries, nothing at all from the curious house of Rimbaud. No hint of a radish. Charpinel's jaundice had begun to abate, and he would soon be able to return to work. Although the fate of Eugène de Pontarche remained a mystery, M. Gour began finally to let his guard down.

On Thursday June 27th—Feast of St. Basilides—he went to the theater.

On his return home, as he was getting ready for bed, he heard a floorboard creak out in the corridor. He eased open his door furtively and spotted a dim light moving at the other end of the long, dark corridor. A man with a torch was moving about the place. The mysterious visitor disappeared into the living room. M. Gour seized a weapon and followed. He flipped the light switch.

But at that moment there came a gunshot. The bullet hit the chandelier and shattered it, along with the light bulb. Then a second bullet struck the wall behind the publisher. Fortunately

for him, the shot went wild. A moment later, M. Gour was thrown
to the floor amid the sound of pounding footsteps. He got up
and ran into his study, intending to telephone for the police.
But the telephone wire had been severed.

After a few minutes' anxious waiting, he convinced himself
that his attacker was gone. When he investigated, he found the
front door hanging open.

A penknife was embedded in the door, holding in place a
leafless pink radish and a business card:

*Arthur Rimbaud and Sons*
*Fruits, Groceries, Seeds,*
*27 rue du Souvenir*
*Roscoff (Finistère)*

Their professional curiosity piqued, the three mystery novelists decided to try and solve the puzzle. One spent his days
consulting newspaper archives; another departed for Brittany;
the third kept a close eye on the Montparnasse station.

And sure enough, something happened which only ever
happens in mystery novels. Where the police failed, the amateur sleuths succeeded. On Sunday, June 30th—the Feast of
St. Martial—the three novelists telephoned M. Gour. They had
something they needed to tell him. They requested a meeting.
That same evening, the publisher welcomed them to his quarters.

Among newspaper clippings dating back some thirty years,
they had found a story dating back to 1913. They invited M.
Gour to read.

He learned that one night in September 1913, a burglary had
been committed at a bank in Roscoff. The value of the theft was
700,000 francs. A night watchman had been mortally wounded,
but before he died he managed to name his killer: Jules Rambaud. It was established that Rambaud had not acted alone.
One of the bank's employees had furnished the thief with the
means of entering the bank. However, the conspirator's identity
was never discovered. When arrested, Rambaud did not betray
his accomplice. He was given a life sentence of hard labor.

The writers then produced press clippings dated November
1934. They reported that a group of convicts, including Jules
Rambaud, had managed to escape from the penal colony.

The connection with the radish affair was obvious. Roscoff...

Rue du Souvenir: so many reminders of the past. Seven hundred thousand radishes meant 700,000 francs. The leaves were there to make matters worse. In some dark corner of Paris, Jules Rambaud was in hiding, sending these absurd messages from "Maison Rimbaud," coded demands for the return of his loot. Apparently, after Rambaud's conviction, his accomplice had made off with the entire 700,000....

"I see," M. Gour concluded. "So he wants the money left for him at Montparnasse station. But why is he targeting me of all people?"

Here, the three novelists looked at each other in some embarrassment. They seemed reluctant to continue, but the publisher insisted. Eventually, they relented.

"M. Gour, about your father... do you know exactly how he made his fortune?"

"His fortune? You're not seriously suggesting that..." he commenced haughtily.

"We mean no disrespect, M. Gour. But... can you answer the question?"

"Well, all right. It's completely ridiculous, but I see no reason not to. Twenty years ago, my father inherited a large sum from a distant relative. He then dabbled in the stock market, and grew his fortune."

"Did you personally know this distant relative?"

"No. I was living abroad at the time."

But the writers did. They had already investigated, and found that there was no way said distant relative could have left a significant legacy—he had ended his days in a hospice, in abject poverty.

They posed one last question to the editor. "What did your father do for a living in 1913?"

"I don't know," answered a distraught M. Gour. "I wasn't on good terms with him and, as I've told you, I wasn't living in France at the time."

"He worked as a security guard at a bank in Roscoff, M. Gour."

"Roscoff...?" stammered the editor.

"The very one where Jules Rambaud committed his crime."

*

That same evening, M. Gour went to Montparnasse station. He soon noticed a bearded figure in a long raincoat who was pacing up and down the platform. Gour approached, and hissed: "Rambaud?"

"Gour?" whispered the man. But he swiftly recoiled, a revolver appearing in his hand. "You're not Gour! You bastard, I'll..."

"I'm his son!" the editor protested. "My father died two and a half years ago."

"So that's why it took you so long to decipher my messages. Well? Where's my money?"

Without a word, M. Gour held out a huge wad of banknotes.

"I'll trust you not to try and short change me," said the convict, stuffing the money into his pockets. "Good-bye."

"Wait! What about Pontarche? What have you done with him?"

"Oh, don't worry about him. He'll be back with you tomorrow, fresh as a daisy."

And with that, the man was gone. He hailed a cab on rue de Rennes, which took him to place du Châtelet. There, he paid his fare and entered a café. In the bathroom, he removed his beard and moustache. Then he headed for a telephone booth, and dialed a number.

"It's done. Did you give Pontarche the sedative?"

"Yes," said the other, "he'll be out for a while."

"Perfect. Now get out, and leave the key in the door. I'll see you at the rendezvous."

*

Later, three men met at the Gare du Nord and boarded the Brussels express.

It was the three mystery novelists. Tired of spending their days inventing ingenious crimes which often went unappreciated, they had decided one day that it might prove more lucrative to turn their fictions into reality.

Launching this ingenious scam had required the use of three elements: the theft of 700,000 francs from a Roscoff bank in 1913; the fact that M. Gour, Senior had worked at said bank; and, finally, Jules Rambaud's escape from the penal colony. But in fact, Gour Senior had nothing whatsoever to do with the theft. He was a man of integrity. He really had inherited a fortune from a distant relative, which he managed to grow thanks to speculation on the stock market.

Using these three details, the three writers had set about defrauding their own publisher—the man who paid their wages.

It seems that mystery novelists have a "different" concept of morality from the rest of us. Case in point: these three observed to their great amusement that pink radishes were on the menu in the restaurant car. They grinned at each other as they ordered.

# SOUPE DU PAPE

"For God's sake," grumbled the Pope, "where the hell has that idiot Oscar put my tobacco?"

Gripping his pungent cherry wood pipe in his teeth, the Pope shuffled through papers and stationery; he ransacked drawers, he searched the pockets of the abandoned jackets and trousers lying about the place.

"Any guesses, Philippe-Auguste?"

Philippe-Auguste did not express an opinion.

In desperation, the Pope grabbed a box of loathsome English tobacco—and inside, there was *his* tobacco, good old-fashioned "grey." He shared his disbelief with Philippe-Auguste. "The man is a lunatic."

Philippe-Auguste growled in agreement, and they both headed for the kitchen.

On the table was a thick paper bag full of peas. The Pope set about shelling them for soup, pluming voluptuous serpents of smoke from his pipe.

Philippe-Auguste stretched out on a nearby chair, yawned, and watched.

Suddenly the Pope stopped what he was doing and let out a curse. "Well I'll be damned... What do you make of that, Philippe-Auguste? This is rather odd...."

He stared in bewilderment at half a dozen peapods in the palm of his hand.

Philippe-Auguste growled once again in reply. Growling and barking were the limits of his conversational talents—Philippe-Auguste was not a man but a sort of pudgy sausage on four stumpy legs: a basset hound.

And while we're at it, you might as well know who the Pope really was. He was a paunchy, heavily mustachioed man of about forty. His name was Bladout. He was one of the best inspectors the *police judiciaire* had ever seen. Indeed, his only flaw was a certain humorlessness. Bladout did not laugh—he did not even smile. He didn't get jokes. Serious as the Pope, that's what his colleagues said. Hence his nickname: the Pope.

Nonetheless, he had been stalked all his life by the relentlessly comical hand of fate.

Of all the names in the world—all the Pauls, Léons and Jules—what do you think his parents called him?

César. Why not Hannibal, or Hector?

But that was not all. As well as a ridiculous name, his parents also gifted little César a brother. Mme Bladout soon gave birth to a second son, Oscar.

Now that their parents were dead, and because they remained bachelors, the brothers had moved in together.

Unfortunately Oscar—unlike César—was an incurable fantasist, his head permanently in the clouds. He drove César to distraction; to the point where César feared he might suffocate under his own suppressed rage. César was decidedly earthbound, with his feet planted firmly on terra firma. Where had his younger brother found their apartment? Rue de la Lune! And what an apartment it was. Triangular, hexagonal, diamond-shaped, star-shaped rooms: designed for a latter-day Dr. Caligari. César, meanwhile, was only comfortable in conventional square rooms.

César had not wanted a dog; Oscar had imposed one on him.

And of course it had to be the most baroque, the most comical, the least "serious" of all dogs—the pudgy sausage: the basset hound. César had wanted to give him a dignified name: Médor, Black, or Sultan. But Oscar baptized the basset Philippe-Auguste.

So it was with everything: César craved order, while Oscar preferred disorder. Clean laundry was found in the bathroom and library, while the dirty linen was neatly piled in the cupboards. Oscar heaped grey tobacco into Craven boxes, kept cognac in the medicine cabinet, and toothpaste in the cocktail cabinet.

César worked—and cooked. Oscar made a nuisance of himself—and played the harmonica. Before bed, César carefully turned out all the lights; when Oscar got home at around two or three in the morning, he could blow a fuse simply by flipping a switch.

At that moment, as he sat with only Philippe-Auguste for company, the Pope shelled his peas with extraordinary feverishness. Each minute he let out a fresh exclamation. "For God's sake! How bizarre. What does it mean? Well I'll be damned..."

Philippe-Auguste paid little attention. From time to time he scratched himself.

When he had finished shelling the peas, the inspector put on his bowler hat and rushed for the stairs. On the third-floor landing he bumped into his brother, who was coming home somewhat hung-over from a night's carousing.

"Unless I'm very much mistaken," he said, "I've stumbled on something very interesting indeed. But I'll get to the bottom of it, don't you worry. Go and finish preparing lunch. I'll be back in an hour."

And he resumed his descent with a sense of haste that did not match his habitual air of dignity. Oscar shrugged and carried on up to the apartment. He said hello to Philippe-Auguste, then went to bed to await César's return. Preparing lunch, no matter how simple, was just not his style.

*

Around the same time, on the second floor of a building in the rue de Cléry, a doorbell chimed. It was answered by a maid, who found herself faced with a man in overalls carrying a toolbox.

"I'm the plumber," he declared.

"So what?" answered the startled maid.

"You mean the concierge didn't warn you? There's a leak somewhere. I've come to check your water meter."

"First I've heard about it," said the maid, who was Belgian. "But you'd better get on with it."

She stepped aside and the man entered the apartment.

"Where's the kitchen?"

"I'll show you."

They headed through a couple of adjoining rooms, where the plumber admired the lavish furnishings. The apartment belonged to an engineer: M. Louis Courlac.

In the kitchen, a stout woman was washing dishes.

"Madeleine," said the maid, "the plumber's here to check the water meter. Apparently there's a leak...."

The cook wiped her hands on her apron, and made way for the apologetic plumber.

"Sorry to disturb you..."

"Don't worry, dear. I've finished the dishes."

The workman took a hammer and a spanner out of the pocket of his overalls and began knocking on the lead pipes, then he unscrewed a tap. The maid left the room.

The cook, however, watched the plumber's progress with interest. He turned to her. "You don't have a stepladder by any chance, do you?"

"I certainly do. Wait here, I'll go and fetch it."

No sooner had she left him than the plumber quickly opened his toolbox. It contained no tools, but instead housed about a kilo of unshelled peas wrapped in newspaper. A similar package lay on the table, which the plumber quickly grabbed and replaced with those he had brought.

"I interrupted you for nothing," he said to the cook on her return with the stepladder. "I've found the problem. It'll take about five minutes to fix."

He screwed the tap back into place.

"And there we are!"

"Care for a drop of Pinard?" the cook suggested.

The plumber drank. "That hits the spot!" he declared jovially.

"What about the bill? Shall I fetch Madame, or will you send it later?"

"No bill. The landlord will take care of it."

He touched his cap and left. The cook began shelling the peas, not once suspecting the strange substitution that had just been made.

*

Half an hour later, Inspector Bladout rushed into the rue Poissonnière police station. A few words were all it took to convince the *commissaire* of the importance of the affair he had stumbled upon.

"It's remarkable," said the bewildered magistrate. "Remarkable!"

Five minutes later, César Bladout left the police station flanked by two officers. They headed for the rue des Petits-Carreaux, where the market was in full swing. The stalls were swamped by housewives laden with shopping bags.

Bladout pointed to one of these merchants: an elderly woman who sold peas and other vegetables.

"That's the one."

The officers approached, pushing their way through the customers. One of them planted a hand on the vendor's shoulder. "Come with us."

"But why, Officer? My papers are all in order, here is my license..."

She showed them a few documents.

"Keep your mouth shut and come with us."

To get things moving, one of the officers grabbed the handles of the vendor's cart and began to push.

"Please, what did I do? What did I do?" cried the frightened old woman.

At the police station, her astonishment changed to amazement when she saw the officers hauling the cart into the interview squad room.

"Get to work, boys!" ordered Bladout.

The officers set about shelling the immense pile of peas, one by one. Even Bladout—even the magistrate!

"My God," the vendor moaned. She wondered whether it was she or they who had gone mad.

        *

Once the extraordinary tale began to spread, the neighborhood was seized by a frenzy. The market was swamped once again. Everyone wanted to buy peas. Naturally, there were not enough. Several vendors had to keep their stock under lock and key.

The streets were no longer safe. Women had their bags snatched—not their handbags but their shopping bags, on the off-chance they might contain peas.

Certain wags hummed the famous tune: *Ah, les p'tits pois, les p'tits pois, les p'tits pois...*

By noon, the press had revealed the cause of this mass hysteria. According to *Les Parisiens*:

*A Remarkable Find!*
*Pearls worth 500,000 francs found in a bag of peas!*

"*Fortune,*" the article began, "*no longer favors the brave but the sheller of peas.*

"*Previously, it seemed that oysters were the only place to find pearls. But this morning, Inspector César Bladout was shelling peas in his kitchen—peas purchased in the rue des Petits-Carreaux, from market vendor Mme Mouffet—when, to his understandable surprise, he found that one of the peapods contained a pearl! Examining the pod carefully, the inspector noticed that it had been opened— likely with a fingernail. This was how the pearl had been secreted inside. But this was not the only surprise in store for Inspector Bladout. Soon he found a second pearl hidden in another pod. Then a third—and so on, until there were a dozen! At first he thought it was some kind of joke. Nevertheless, he presented his find to M. Bloch, a jeweler on boulevard Bonne Nouvelle. M. Bloch was in no doubt: the pearls were real, and of considerable value. M. Bloch estimates their combined value at half a million francs. Mme Mouffet claims to know nothing about them, and it is hard to dispute her story— after all, if she were responsible for the theft, surely she would not have sold the pearls for two francs a pound! Indeed, police have reason to believe that those twelve pearls were the only ones, because soon after the inspector's discovery the remaining stock of peas was examined without result. Evidently, these pearls are stolen jewelry. The pea pods must have appealed to the criminal as a perfect means of removing his loot from its owner's property unnoticed.*

*"But he did not anticipate the ill fortune that would thwart his plans! Inspector César Bladout is now in charge of the investigation. As soon as the rightful owner of the pearls has been identified, the identity of the culprit will likely soon be revealed. Several domestic servants are currently being questioned."*

In the kitchens of the many houses around the boulevard Bonne-Nouvelle and the rues Poissonnière, Saint-Denis, and Réaumur, countless residents spent hours shelling peas with no intention of eating them.

But they did not find a single pearl.

"This is an absurd business," growled the Pope.

He had finished polishing his black shoes, and was now brushing his jacket and bowler hat.

Oscar Bladout, meanwhile, had debuted his "summer" wardrobe, although it was only the beginning of June: linen trousers, a short-sleeved shirt, sandals on his bare feet, and no hat.

With his hands in his pockets and his pipe in his mouth, the Pope looked as though he were going to a funeral. The basset hound Philippe-Auguste stood between his feet.

"Absurd! Everything about this case is ridiculous. It's a farce. I'm disoriented. I feel out of place, like I've put on one of your suits by mistake."

Oscar laughed.

Contrary to expectation, the rightful owner of the pearls had not yet come forward. Not even with half a million francs at stake! Perhaps they had been the victim of another, more violent crime....

The inquiries among domestic servants and employment agencies yielded nothing. Giving Mme Mouffet the third degree proved useless. Thinking that the owner might have lost her pearls while out on the town, investigators started making the rounds of restaurants, ranging from bistros where the onion soup costs thirty sous to the chic clubs where it costs six francs. All without success.

Night after night the inspector wandered thoughtfully among heaps of peas, carrots, turnips, cabbages, lettuces, slipping on leaves, crushing tomatoes. People gossiped as he passed: "There's the policeman who found those pearls in his peas!"

Bladout was annoyed. His years of experience had not prepared him for this. He was not used to it.

He was the butt of every joke at the police station. They even made fun of him at the Café du Palais, where he liked to go for a quiet drink, and to smoke his pipe.

The supplier who provided Mme Mouffet with her vegetables got them from Arpajon. So, the Pope went to Arpajon. And, looking like a mourner in an invisible funeral procession, he wandered once again among Himalaya-sized heaps of vegetables.

Nothing. Not a single thing.

"Stop for a moment and think," Oscar told him one day.

"I don't *think*," protested the Pope. "That's not my method. I investigate. I wait. And, finally, I understand. But this time I think I must admit defeat...."

"Listen. Here's a strange point. When Mme Mouffet served you the kilo of peas, she grabbed them by the handful at random, didn't she? So how did she come to give you the twelve pods with pearls in them? It seems an incredible coincidence! Wouldn't it make more sense if they *didn't* come from Mme Mouffet's stall at all, and the thief had in fact planted them directly in your bag—while you were paying for your purchase, for example."

"But why?"

"Perhaps he was being chased by the owner, or by an accomplice?"

"Utterly ridiculous," said Inspector Bladout, shrugging his broad shoulders.

He went into the kitchen and began to make coffee. For lunch, the two men had eaten boudin, which had left traces stuck to the bottom of the pan. There was also a smell of grease, so the inspector opened the window before he tied a blue apron around his waist and began to wash the dishes.

By the time César Bladout was leaving for work, a light rain had begun to fall. He searched around for his trench coat, but couldn't find it.

That idiot Oscar must have taken it by accident when he went out earlier. The Pope had to resort to Oscar's raincoat, which was predictably ridiculous. It was made from the same flimsy material as a tobacco pouch, and, to top it off, it was bright green.

Walking along the rue de Cléry, the Pope crossed paths with a heavyset woman.

*I'm sure I've seen her before...*

He had a good memory for faces, and quickly identified the passer-by.

*A maid, or a cook... Wait! She was at the market in the rue des Petits-Carreaux!*

He growled. He felt terribly uncomfortable in the green raincoat. He felt as though all eyes were on him in this absurd garment.

"That idiot Oscar."

And suddenly Inspector César Bladout, otherwise known as the Pope, stopped short.

"Dear God! I've got it!"

He remembered perfectly. The woman he had just seen was also at Mme Mouffet's stall when he was buying the peas. She was buying salad, but she also had a packet of peas. While getting out his wallet, the inspector had placed his own packet on the cart. Had he inadvertently grabbed this woman's peas instead of his own? But if *she* had bought them from Mme Mouffet, then all his questions still remained.

But perhaps she had bought them elsewhere? If so, a whole new angle for his investigation had come to light.

Bladout caught up with the woman.

"One moment please, my lovely!"

"You rude pig. Do you want me to give you a slap?"

"Police. Shut up and come with me."

He took her to the station.

Within ten minutes he had the whole story.

"My name is Madeleine Peclet. I am a cook for M. Louis Courlac, an engineer, who lives on rue de Cléry."

Like everybody else, she well remembered the infamous Day of the Peas. She remembered it all the better, she declared, because that morning a plumber had visited M. Courlac's house under the pretext of checking the water pressure, though the concierge had later informed her that no plumber had been sent. The man was an impostor!

However, nothing had been reported missing from the Courlac residence.

"Your peas... Where did you buy them? From Mme Mouffet?"

"No, sir. I didn't buy them. It was my friend Maria Martin who gave them to me. Maria is a cook in the same building as me. She works for a crazy American called Mme Stockfeld."

"Crazy? How so?"

"If you were as rich as she is, would *you* live on the rue de Cléry?"

"She's that rich?"

"Even *she* doesn't know how rich she is!"

"Go on."

"Well, that morning I went for my walk. On the way, I stopped at Mme Stockfeld's to see if Maria wanted to come shopping with me. She told me no, because Madame was leaving that morning for Italy, so no one would be eating there that day. That reminded her that she had a kilo of peas that would go to waste, and did I want them? Four francs' worth, she said, and if I gave them to my boss I might get a bonus. So I took the peas."

"Thank you, my dear," Bladout beamed. "Does Mme Stockfeld still live with her husband?"

"No, sir. She is a widow."

"So she lives alone?"

"No, she has a butler and a secretary. They live in the apartment, too." Bladout frowned, and the cook gave him a cheeky pout. "She's a decrepit old thing of fifty, and the butler and secretary are both twenty-five. So it balances out, if you see what I mean."

"Indeed. And what are these young chaps called?"

"The butler is William. He's English. The secretary is Hernando Miguel y Alvarez y... I don't know what. One of those weird long names. He's Argentinian. All three of them have gone to Italy."

"I see, I see. Well, you may go now, my girl," said the Pope with a benevolent gesture.

Everything had become clear. One of Mme Stockfeld's lovers was the thief. And the American widow's silence was explained by her travels abroad—she did not yet even know that she was a victim of theft.

"God bless Oscar," exclaimed the Pope. "If he hadn't picked

up my trench coat by mistake, I never would have realised that I picked up the wrong peas!"

William was a strapping lad with a face the color of raw beef. Señor Hernando Miguel y Alvarez y etc. was lean and lithe as a serpent, with dark skin, a limp handshake, and a slithery gaze.

On their return from Italy, both men were questioned, and soon confessed.

Both of them.

For each man had committed theft on his own account. The operation was accomplished in two stages. First of all, Hernando Miguel y Alvarez y etc. stole the pearls. He hid them in a vase. But William, who had also been eyeing the jewels, saw him and, in turn, stole them from the thief. But before he could make a run for it, there came sudden, frantic cries from Mme Stockfeld's bedroom.

William wondered what the matter could be. Of course, Mme Stockfeld had discovered the theft! (In reality, she was calling for help simply because one of her Pekinese had soiled the carpet.)

William's immediate concern was to ensure he was not caught with the pearls in his possession. At that moment, he was in the kitchen. He was alone. He saw the peas. A stroke of genius: he would hide the pearls there! With the emergency over, he returned—but the peas were gone. Maria, the cook, explained that she gave them to her friend Madeleine. So William sent an accomplice to play the plumber at the Courlac residence, and to substitute the peas. But the scheme failed, fate having already put Inspector Bladout in possession of the pearls, thanks to another involuntary substitution—this time, at Mme Mouffet's cart.

"I am very much obliged to you, Detective," said Mme Stockfeld in her thick Chicago accent. "I'm infinitely grateful. But please—do me one last favor. Give them back to me."

"What do you mean? You already have the pearls back."

"Not the pearls. *Them*."

She was requesting the return of William and Señor Hernando Miguel y Alvarez y etc.

"I do not wish to press charges. And as a token of my gratitude, Inspector, I would like you to accept these two pearls. You may keep a quarter of their value by way of reward, and I would like the rest to go to the police benevolent fund."

Fortunately, William and Hernando Miguel etc. had no prior

convictions. And so they returned to their mistress. She took them in with a gaze that was more affectionate than stern.

"My boys," she said, "my wicked, wicked boys. I forgive you."

*

Some time later, César and Oscar Bladout were vacationing in Cancale, in a bizarre Etruscan-style pavilion discovered by the indescribable Oscar.

"I've taken care of breakfast," he said one morning.

"You have? Will wonders never cease. And what have you prepared?"

"Nothing. I bought some oysters."

"Did you open them, at least?"

"I thought I'd leave that for you."

With a groan, the inspector began to open the oysters.

In the first, he found a pea. And in the second, another pea. And so on.

Oscar was clutching his sides, positively howling with laughter.

"That's very funny," said César, serious as the Pope.

# THE MYSTERY OF THE GREEN ROOM

The wallpaper was old pink.

The drawing room wallpaper, of course. In the bedroom, inevitably, it was green; a rich green Trianon.

"Yes, gentlemen," declared Madame Emilienne de Rouvres, "it was about two in the morning. I was asleep. Then, suddenly…"

Haunted by the memory of this "sudden" incident, Madame de Rouvres shuddered. Her two listeners, seated opposite, shuddered along with her, as a mark of respect. One was Inspector Jean Martin of the *police judiciaire*; the other, the private detective Marcel Fermier, was currently employed by the Sirius Agency, from whom Madame de Rouvres had purchased fire and theft insurance.

It was ten o'clock in the morning. Only the squealing brakes of a passing *triporteur* disturbed the tranquility of the rue des Sablons.

"Suddenly," resumed Madame de Rouvres, "there was a creak in the hallway that woke me up. I turned on the light. 'Who's there?' No answer. 'Who is it?' Silence. I live alone, gentlemen, and I don't keep a weapon in the house. All the same, I got up and walked over to the bedroom door. There was a masked man standing there. Before I had time to cry out, he pounced…."

With almost comical synchronicity, the expressions of the inspector and the private detective displayed a broad gamut of emotions: admiration of Mme de Rouvres' bravery, anxiety at the danger, and horrified contemplation of the barbaric attack.

For her part, Mme de Rouvres' face was heavily made up and flushed with emotion. It almost matched the wallpaper. An irreverent type might have called her mutton dressed as lamb.

Not that she was old. She was "just over forty." Then she was "in her forties." Finally, she was "hardly more than fifty."

She was an individual of excellent breeding and considerable wealth, who must have been very attractive around 1910—just as her drawing room must have been in the days when it boasted carefully-selected Louis XVI furnishings.

Alas, they had all been auctioned long ago. The genuine Aubusson armchairs and marquetry rosewood cabinets were gone now. Only one symbol of the good old days remained: the pink wallpaper. Alas, Mme de Rouvres' face had also fallen victim to time, the pitiless auctioneer of beauty.

Only the sparkle in her eyes and the pinkness in her cheeks remained—enhanced by kohl and make-up, of course.

"So, madame," said Marcel Fermier, "this individual attacked you, he knocked you out...."

"No, monsieur," Mme de Rouvres corrected him with an ambiguous pout, "no, he didn't knock me out! He gagged me, tied me up, and sat me down on a stool in the hallway."

"Then," ventured Jean Martin, "he went into the green room?"

"No, Inspector," Mme de Rouvres corrected once again, "he didn't go into the green room. He went into the dining room, and ransacked my silverware. Then he came into this very drawing room and set his sights on a clock and two silver candlesticks. After that..."

Mme de Rouvres got up, pushed aside a screen, and lifted a tapestry to reveal a small wall safe. It had been forced open.

"As well as a few private papers, this safe contained three thousand francs. The thief took them, of course."

"And what about your jewelry?"

"I don't keep that in here. I always assume burglars are drawn to safes like flies. I keep my jewelry in the drawer of my bedside table."

The same method used by Poe in "The Purloined Letter," thought Fermier. The best way to hide an object is not to hide it all....

He asked, "And when he left the drawing room, is that when he went to the green room and snatched your jewelry?"

"Thank God," Mme de Rouvres said with a deep sigh, "my jewels are safe. The thief didn't go into my bedroom at all. The fool just took a peek in through the door, then he left with the clock, the candlesticks, the silverware and the three thousand francs. I had to wait until eight o'clock—that is to say, when my housekeeper arrived—before I could be untied."

*

Once Mme de Rouvres had retired to the green room again, the two men commenced their investigation of the apartment.

"This breaks every single rule," growled Fermier.

"What?" said Martin. "What breaks the rules?"

"This burglary. Why didn't the thief go into the green room?"

Martin gestured vaguely. "I don't see what's so surprising about it. The green room used to be Louis XV, and the drawing room used to be Louis XVI. But apart from the sofa, the bedside table, and the chairs, the only thing left is the wallpaper."

"What about the jewelry? Everyone knows Mme de Rouvres owns a pearl necklace and a vast array of valuable diamonds. Supposedly eight hundred thousand francs' worth!"

"A pretty penny," said Martin.

"Those jewels are all that's left of Mme de Rouvres' fortune. She's so enamored of them that she'd rather see her antique furniture, her rugs, and her paintings go one by one, and lead a more modest lifestyle. Everybody knows that. The thief must have known it too."

"All right," grumbled an irritated Martin, "so we're dealing with an amateur. That's obvious, or else he would have guessed the jewelry was in the drawer of the bedside table...."

The methods of the two investigators were profoundly different. Martin, a big man with a moustache, applied all the principles that had been instilled in him by the *police judiciaire*. He scoured the furniture, the mantelpieces, the safe, the dresser drawers; he scrutinized the parquet floors; he studied the lock on the front door. He searched methodically for footprints, or some other clue.

Footprints, fingerprints, cigarette butts, saliva. He even sniffed like a bloodhound. But he wasn't searching for the inescapable scent of violets that Mme de Rouvres loved so much, and which permeated the apartment. He was after a much more vulgar smell, very different from perfume—except to a dog, perhaps. One of the things the *police judiciaire* had taught him was that many burglars cannot resist leaving behind them an excremental "autograph." But nowhere did he perceive the presence of this distinctly Gallic calling card. He surmised: "No excrement: our man must be of a moderately high social level. No fingerprints: he wore gloves."

Fermier, planting himself in the center of each room, limited his activity to a slow pivot on one heel. His gaze took in each piece of furniture in turn.

He was a skinny, bespectacled young man. He was also a bookworm, who tended to apply the literary methods of Chevalier Dupin, Poe's fictional hero.

While the policeman looked for clues, Fermier tried to pinpoint the motive. To him, the theft of the clock, the candlesticks, the silverware, and the three thousand francs seemed derisory.

From time to time, Martin threw a sardonic sideways glance in the young man's direction. Then, somewhat impatiently, he plunged his hand into his jacket pocket and lovingly caressed the bowl of his pipe. It was not a sense of propriety inspired by the mistress of the house that kept him from smoking. Rather, it was respect for the Louis XV and Louis XVI décor—most of which was gone anyway, but which remained in the form of the old pink and green Trianon wallpapers.

Suddenly, Fermier approached him.

"Have you read *The Mystery of the Yellow Room*, by Gaston Leroux?"

Martin shook his head. "You really think I can afford to waste time reading novels?"

"Hey, it's not always a waste of time."

Martin shrugged.

"In the book," Fermier continued, "Leroux poses what's known as a 'locked-room mystery.'"

Martin chuckled. "I know what you're talking about. A hermetically sealed room, under surveillance at all times, which cannot be entered or exited without being seen... and yet the killer pulls it off anyway. That sort of nonsense is all very well in fiction, but in reality... Anyway, what's the connection?"

"Well, it strikes me that the mystery of the green room is comparable to that of the *Yellow Room*, in the sense that it is the exact opposite. It's what you might call an '*un*locked room mystery.' Here, the thief could have entered and exited the green room without difficulty, and yet..."

Martin laughed. "And yet he didn't bother! Is that what you mean? Doesn't take much to keep you entertained, does it?"

Fermier continued his meditations a moment longer, then Martin decided to examine the jewels. They were splendid. The inspector was dazzled. Near the window, in the bright light of the June morning, Fermier also admired the jewels then returned them to their owner.

Shortly afterward, the inspector and the private detective left. Martin was sullen. This case did not interest him; he preferred bloody murders and crimes of passion. *They* were worthy of his talents, and gave him a chance to demonstrate his sleuthing flair.

But this piddling little burglary was a job for beginners, at best.

Fermier, on the other hand, seemed particularly intrigued.

He quoted in oratorical tones: "Has the necklace lost nothing of its charm, nor the jewels their brightness?"

Martin blenched. "What are you talking about?"

"Nothing. Simply paraphrasing a passage from the Yellow Room, about a presbytery and a garden."

Martin eyed the private detective with pity. "You poor fellow," he said.

Fermier looked at his watch. "Eleven-thirty. What do you say to an aperitif?"

They settled on a café terrace.

The Pernod slowly changed color as the lumps of sugar and ice melted in the sun. Pretty young women in skimpy dresses drifted past, and Martin sat back to enjoy the free show.

"There *is* an explanation for the mystery of the green room," the private detective said suddenly. "Suppose Mme de Rouvres' jewels were fake..."

"Huh?"

"I said: suppose that at some point, without Mme de Rouvres' knowledge, the jewels were replaced with a convincing set of fakes. And while we're at it, suppose the burglar *knew* about the replacement. *That's* why he didn't go into the green room. What would be the point, if he knew the jewels were fake?"

"You're too imaginative for your own good," the inspector retorted.

Fermier's eyes flashed mischievously behind his tortoiseshell spectacles. He checked his watch again.

"Damn! One o'clock already! Time to eat red meat!"

Not having read *The Mystery of the Yellow Room*, Martin could not have known that Fermier was once again paraphrasing a line from Leroux's famous novel. He took the quip at face value, and answered seriously: "Lucky you. I've been sentenced to a lifetime of white meat."

Then he began chattering about bellyache, heartburn, etc. Fermier was only half-listening.

They parted. After about a hundred paces, the inspector looked back. He saw the private detective standing still in front of a second-hand bookstore. Indulging his passion, Fermier fondled grubby, germ-laden books.

All that reading will drive him mad, Martin thought.

That afternoon, the inspector had a few visits to make—unrelated to "the mystery of the green room." As he walked, he passed milliners', furriers', tailors' and glove-makers' shops, almost all of them empty of customers.

More unlocked-room mysteries, he thought.

*

But Inspector Martin would discover that the private detective was indeed onto something. In fact, the investigation of the burglary in the rue des Sablons was soon to take an unexpected turn.

Mme de Rouvres had the idea of taking her pearls and diamonds to the jeweler who, many years ago, had sold them to her in the first place. After the examination, she received the horrifying news: they were fake.

She lodged an official complaint against the unknown thief, and sent the Sirius Agency a formal claim for the indemnity provided by the insurance policy.

"I'm afraid the agency is going to make things difficult," Fermier confided to Martin.

"Why?"

"Because," said the private investigator wryly, "this case is a little too similar to the Yellow Room. Similar in the sense that it's the exact opposite."

"Very funny," Martin retorted gruffly.

"I'm not joking."

"All right, so explain yourself."

"It's simple. I discovered a kind of parallel between the two cases. In Leroux's novel, the malefactor enters the Yellow Room in spite of all the obstacles in his way. However, in *this* case the malefactor..."

"Doesn't enter the green room, in spite of the open door. You already told me that. What else?"

"What else? Why, the parallels continue. In the case of the Yellow Room, the malefactor convinces everyone that the crime which he committed earlier was actually committed *later*. Conversely, in the affair of the pearls and the diamonds, I get the impression that someone wanted us to think that the crime they had not yet committed had already happened."

"Who, for God's sake?"

"Madame de Rouvres, of course!"

"Have you gone mad?"

"Think about it, Inspector. Mme de Rouvres is far from wealthy. In fact, she needs money. Little by little, armchair by armchair, table by table, she had to give up her Louis XV bedroom and her Louis XVI drawing room. And still she needs money. There is only one option left: to sell her jewelry. But Mme de Rouvres does not want to do that. She can't bear the idea.

"Therefore, she has a secret set of copies made. She arranges a fake burglary. That is to say, she breaks into her safe, steals three thousand francs, a clock, some silver candlesticks and cutlery. After that, when we show up at her house, she draws our attention to the fact that the thief did *not* enter the green room. Why did she do that? To make us think that the thief didn't want the jewelry.

"This was to make us suspect the jewels were fake, and to conclude that the real ones had already been stolen long ago. I admit, that's exactly what I concluded.

"Everything else proceeds according to plan. Mme de Rouvres visits the jeweler. She discovers that the jewels are fake, she lodges a complaint, and files for compensation from the insurance company. A policy worth around four hundred thousand francs. Well worth spending a few hours tied up—not too tightly!—on a stool in the hallway."

"It's very complicated, but it's not so stupid, this theory of yours," murmured the inspector. "The staged burglary would make Mme de Rouvres seem like the least likely suspect."

He thought for a moment. "Unless..."

"Unless?"

"I can think of another suspect: the jeweler, who sold her the diamonds and pearls in the first place. He was in a better position than anyone to produce copies. Let's say *he* staged the burglary. Then all he has to do is wait for Mme de Rouvres to bring the jewels in for him to examine. He makes the exchange, and *voil*à. Who would suspect him?"

"It's possible," Fermier nodded. "But either way, how do we prove it?"

*

Four days later, Inspector Martin found the proof. During a search of the jeweler's cellar he discovered Mme de Rouvres' clock, candlesticks and silverware under a heap of cardboard boxes.

As expected, the jeweler protested his innocence, asserted that he did not know how those objects had come to be there, and insisted that he had been framed.

He was arrested anyway. All the same, the real jewels remained elusive.

Fermier, however, did not hide his feelings from the inspector. He was by no means convinced of the jeweler's guilt, and still suspected Mme de Rouvres.

"*She* could have hidden the clock and the candlesticks in the jeweler's cellar!"

"Don't be stupid! This isn't something out of a novel."

Ten days went by.

Fermier kept a close eye on Mme de Rouvres' home. He persisted for a while, even though no discoveries were forthcoming.

Finally, at about three o'clock one afternoon, Martin approached him while he was watching from the rond-point de Longchamp.

"No luck yet? I admire your stubbornness!"

"Well, my friend, as long as the jewels are still missing, I think we ought to give the jeweler the benefit of the doubt."

Beaming condescendingly, Martin slipped an arm around the private investigator's shoulders.

"I wasn't just passing, you know. I've come to relieve you of duty."

"What do you mean?"

"You're right: the jeweler is innocent. He's just been released. But get *this*: Mme de Rouvres is innocent, too."

"Have you got proof?"

"The best! I managed to lay my hands on the jewels. The real ones."

"Where did you find them?" Fermier was startled.

"Very funny! Are you really asking me? I found them in your rooms, carefully hidden under a floorboard."

The private detective had turned pale.

Martin hailed a passing cab.

"Take us to the *police judiciaire.*"

The two men climbed in.

"You see, Fermier, it was a bad idea to draw my attention to the parallels between this case and that of the Yellow Room. I bought the book, you see, and I—the man who never reads—read it.

"That's when an idea came to me. A crazy idea. *What if we took these parallels to their natural conclusion?* I said to myself. *What if the Mystery of the Green Room turns out to be the complete opposite of* The Mystery of the Yellow Room? I tried to imagine what that would look like.

"And my goodness, it looked rather strange indeed.

"In *the Yellow Room,* there is a private detective and an official inspector. The latter is the culprit. For a perfect parallel, it would be necessary for the policeman (that is to say, me) to be innocent, while the private detective, Fermier, is guilty.

"This conclusion gave me a chuckle, to begin with. Then I thought, why not? It was perfectly conceivable. You stole the clock and the candlesticks. The next day, while pretending to examine the jewels, you substituted them for the fakes right under my nose. After that, you uttered the mysterious phrase: *Has the necklace lost nothing of its charm, nor the jewels their brightness?* Next you directed my suspicions toward a thief from the distant past, then toward Mme de Rouvres. In turn, I considered the jeweler a possible suspect. You immediately went and hid the stolen items in his cellar. Finally, for added authenticity, you continued tailing Mme de Rouvres....

"I probably wouldn't have worked out the solution anytime soon if you hadn't insisted on drawing my attention to the Yellow Room. By the way, I hope you appreciate that thanks to me the parallel between the two cases is going to remain perfect."

"What do you mean?"

With a bark of laughter, Martin explained: "In the *Yellow Room,* at the end of the book, the amateur detective lets the murderous policeman escape justice. It is therefore vital that the opposite happens today: that the policeman does *not* let the amateur detective escape. And you can be sure that he won't."

Handcuffs snapped around Fermier's wrists.

"I told you, didn't I," said a melancholy Fermier, "that reading novels isn't always a waste of time."

# THE KILLER

For a long time the killer had crawled through the weeds and wild carrots, and only a slight undulation of the tall stems betrayed his approach as he climbed into the garden of the isolated house. A delicious freshness reigned there, between the clumps of boxwood, the currant bushes, and the blackcurrants. The killer stood undecided for a moment, wiping his sweaty face with his sleeve, removing the leaves and twigs which clung to him. Then, cautiously, he approached the house and examined its exterior. It was deserted.

The killer only had to touch the door for it to swing silently open. It was a one-story cottage in the middle of nowhere. The furniture was basic. The killer, finding no one at home, collapsed into a chair with a sigh of relief. His face, which was as ruddy as a farmhand's, expressed despair rather than cruelty.

Yes, he had killed; but how was he to know the fellow had a skull like a hazelnut? "Could have fooled me!" he said in the aftermath. He hadn't thought a man could die from a single blow. And because one glass of liquor had led inevitably to another, and mixing one's drinks is always a disaster, he ended up on the wrong side of the law. He kept quiet: the jury thought him "sly" and "dangerous." Because he was drunk, they took him for an alcoholic. A merciful judge sentenced him to a few years behind bars....

It doesn't matter how exactly this sullen lout managed to escape from the prison transport vehicle a week ago.

What matters is that he was there, in that temporarily deserted house, whose owners had gone to market and would be back by nightfall.

He had spent hundreds of hours wandering the forest, sustaining himself thanks to nocturnal marauding, hunted by police, by civilians, by dogs... and now he had a good three hours to himself. In a cupboard he found wine, cheese, and bread. He ate slowly and drank in moderation. He picked at the bread methodically, and pricked bits of Roquefort with the tip of his knife. Little by little, he grew numb to the suffering within him. His hunger satisfied, the killer put away the bread, the plate and the glass, the bottle with its cork carefully replaced, and a bowl he had found lying around. The killer was an orderly fellow. He was about to doze off when he felt his chair wobble beneath him.

One of its legs had come loose. The act of straightening it, and securing it with a nail, was almost a game for the industrious murderer. The killer liked to tinker. Then he turned his attention to a latch with a badly secured bolt.

Energized by these menial tasks, the killer went out into the back garden and found it badly maintained. He criticized the methods of cultivation, the choice of plants, the placement of the espaliers. "Too many trees!" he said to himself. "The potatoes aren't getting enough sun." Thus, he stalked the plant beds, expressing his opinions aloud, scolding an invisible interlocutor: "They should have rowed those peas... tied those escaroles...." Here and there, he pulled weeds.

A little later, when four gendarmes tiptoed into the garden with revolvers in hand, the killer did not hear them. He was too busy driving a shovel into the earth, eagerly tilling a patch of soil which had been left fallow, where he might have grown excellent cucumbers if he'd only had the chance....

# A LESSON IN CRIME

"Student Lacroix, what can you tell me about Mademoiselle Stangerson's secret?"

"Mademoiselle Stangerson's secret... Uh... Mademoiselle Stangerson's secret..."

"I see that you don't know the first word of it. Come on! Tell me the famous phrase Rouletabille heard in the gardens of the Elysée, behind the wall abutting the Avenue Marigny."

"..."

"Tell me the phrase Rouletabille heard at the Donjon Inn..."

"..."

"I see you haven't even opened your Gaston Leroux. You will copy out thirty times: 'The presbytery has lost nothing of its charm nor the garden its brightness' and 'We shall have to eat red meat—now.' You may sit down. Student Mercier, what do *you* know of Mademoiselle Stangerson's secret?"

"Mademoiselle Stangerson, sir, having secretly married in Philadelphia one Jean Roussel—who was none other than the sinister bandit Ballmeyer, alias detective Frédéric Larsan, alias 'the great Fred,' sir—had a son named Joseph Josephin, subsequently known as Joseph Rouletabille."

"Good. And what was the first material clue discovered by Joseph Rouletabille in *the Yellow Room*?"

"A woman's blond hair, sir."

"Where did the reporter find that hair?"

"Under the bed, sir."

"What did he deduce from it?"

"He deduced Mademoiselle Stangerson's Nightmare, sir."

"Recite Mademoiselle Stangerson's Nightmare. Begin at: *And suddenly, while the cuckoo...*"

"*And, suddenly, while the cuckoo was sounding the half after midnight, a desperate clamor broke out in 'The Yellow Room'. It was the voice of Mademoiselle, crying 'Murder!—murder!—help!' Immediately afterwards revolver shots rang out....*"

"Thank you. Student Jozont, tell me the name of Sherlock Holmes's mortal enemy."

"Professor Moriarty, sir."

"And the date of the widow Lerouge's murder, from 'The Lerouge Affair,' by Gaboriau?"

"March fourth, 1862, sir."

Which policeman managed to solve the mystery?

"Père Tabaret," answered Tirauclair.

"Thank you. Student Charantac, what can you tell me about Isidore Bautrelet?"

"In *The Hollow Needle* the schoolboy Isidore Bautrelet was Arsène Lupin's formidable adversary, sir. He realized that the corpse on the cliff..."

*

This scene takes place in a French high school around the year 2500.

Crime fiction, which was incorporated into baccalaureate programs in the 2300s, gradually took precedence over all other forms of literature, which fell into disrepute and then into obscurity. Edgar Allan Poe, Émile Gaboriau, Gaston Leroux, Maurice Leblanc, Conan Doyle, Edgar Wallace and certain specialized authors from the beginning of the twentieth century have become classics which are studied from seventh grade onwards.

Each student owns a history of the French and foreign detective novel, a book of selected pieces with glossary and commentaries, a précis of police technique, a summary of the Penal Code and the Code of Criminal Instruction, a manual of exercises, and a police dictionary: the *Locard*.

From the morning class:

"*Precisely at six o'clock, as he had foretold, Herlock Sholmes, dressed in trousers that were too short and a coat that was too small, which he had borrowed from an innkeeper at Neuilly...*"

This is dictation.

"*The detective took him by the arm. 'Rest assured,' said he, coolly. 'We'll find the man, or my name's not Lecoq.'*"

This is grammar.

"Get out your *Murder of Roger Ackroyd*, page 269, chapter xxiii: Poirot's Little Reunion: "*And now,*" said Caroline, rising, "*that child is coming upstairs to lie down,*'" to "*What is it?*" I asked."

This is English class.

And so on until lunchtime.

After school, the children ask their parents rather strange questions.

"Maman," the eldest daughter inquires at the dinner table,

while struggling with her beefsteak, "suppose you wanted to poison Papa."

"I'll try," says Maman.

"You only have arsenic."

"All right."

"Where would you slip the poison so he wouldn't taste it?" Papa looks up, waiting for the answer.

"Well," says Maman, "I think very strong coffee would do."

"No, no!" says Papa. "That won't do, my dear! I'd notice it right away! If it were me, I'd wait until the weather turns cold. You know the cold weather gives me heartburn, and I take Brewer's Yeast. Well, you could slip the arsenic into the Brewer's Yeast...."

After the meal, it is the youngest child's turn.

"Maman, in sewing class we have to stitch a balaclava, and braid a rope ladder. Will you show me how?"

"You mean you don't know? A big girl like you! Dear, oh dear!"

Sighing, Maman gets up and fetches her thread, her needles, her scissors, and some rags.

"To cut a balaclava, you start by working out your hem..."

Upstairs a boy stares at the ceiling and yawns, ignoring the open book in front of him and chewing on the lid of his pen.

"You call that studying?" his father shouts. "Is this why I work myself to the bone to give you a decent education?"

The boy looks back at his book and begins to study his criminal investigation course.

Then, back to school.

On the blackboard, teachers draw shapes and numbers.

"If locked-room Y is shaped like an isosceles triangle ABC and locked-room Z is a hexagon MNOPQR, calculate..."

This is geometry class.

"If a safe is lined with a steel plate $x$ millimeters thick, and a blowtorch can cut through $h$ millimeters, calculate the length of time taken to cut through a circular lock with a diameter of..."

This is physics class.

"Tell me the formula of an invisible ink which will reappear after two hours' exposure to sunlight..."

This is chemistry class.

"I'd like you to draw a parquet floor with a corpse on it...."

This is art class.

"Translate the following cryptogram: 20376525434448876

789010107614190512233976101098103434 using the Square Number Method."

This is mathematics class.

At last! Recess.

Kids gather and chat while strolling around the schoolyard.

"Who did you have as the culprit on that logic test?"

"The *juge d'instruction*, of course!"

"Don't be stupid, it's the policeman! Remember the cigarette butt..."

"Not at all," interrupts a third, "it's an alibi trick. The victim was in cahoots with the killer."

Behind the bike sheds, a group of students forms a circle around a gym teacher.

"This exercise is all about climbing through a window in a freshly plastered wall without leaving a trace. You do it in four stages. First stage: bend the knees, hands on hips, keep your back straight..."

Again, we are in the study room.

A murmur of young voices drifts through the open windows.

*Listen, people of France,*
*Of the Kingdom of Chile,*
*People of Russia too,*
*From the Cape of Good Hope*
*The memorable occurrence*
*Of a very serious crime...*

This is music class. Thirty voices are belting out "The Lament of Fualdès." The week before, they were belting out "The Lament of Troppmann." Next week, they'll be belting out "The Lament of Landru."

In a nearby boarding school, young girls belt out "La Paimpolaise," the lament of Violette Nozière:

*To each question Violette answers:*
*Yes, I'm the only culprit*
*I swear to you, Mr President!*
*No one else is responsible*
*For the poisoning of my parents...*

And classes resume.

Philosophy:
"Gentlemen, the affective states in Arsène Lupin..."
Latin:
"Gentlemen, the old adage: Is *fecit cui prodest...*"
Zoology:
"Gentlemen, the definition of the term 'card shark'..."
Literature:
"Gentlemen, the 'Triangle,' in literature, comprises three main characters: the victim, the killer and the detective. There are thirty-two dramatic situations...."
Geography:
"Gentlemen, the French police departments, in descending order of importance from the point of view of criminology, are..."
History:
"Gentlemen, the admission of Vidocq into the *Sûreté...*"
That evening, at home:
"Maman, suppose you murdered your lover with a sickle."
"All right."
"You don't want to be caught."
"All right."
"The police have your description."
"Perfect."
"How would you shake the bloodhounds? Would you wear a wig? Would you leave Paris on foot, by bicycle or by car? Would you take a train? And if so, which station, heading in which direction?"
"Papa, imagine a hallway with seven doors. A millionaire is asleep in the back bedroom. The door and window are locked on the inside. His secretary is keeping watch in the adjoining room. How would you break into the millionaire's house, murder him, rob him, then escape without getting caught?"
Papa thinks for a moment, then gets annoyed. "Too easy! It's a locked-room mystery. There are a bunch of solutions. I could try the Inexplicable Gallery, or the *Odeur Funèbre*. Or I could try... You know, I used to have all the locked-room solutions at my fingertips once upon a time, but I haven't picked up a textbook in so long. Ask your brother."
Children pour their blood, sweat, and tears into these problems. They haul their schoolbags full of books with off-putting titles like *The Strange Death of Sir Jeroboam Backdrive*,

*The Triple Murder in rue Sebastien-Bottin, The Affair of the Red Ears,* and *The Talking Ghost of Talafeix.*

These books are now deathly dull. Since they have been studied, dissected, and commented upon, they are now colder than the corpses they contain.

The deductions of Chevalier Dupin, M. Lecoq, Sherlock Holmes—boring! So boring, Mademoiselle Stangerson's Nightmare, Arsène Lupin's monologue in the fifth act of *813*—those centuries-old tales that play out endlessly at the Odeon and the Français.

Schoolchildren have long since stopped reading thrillers for pleasure. They no longer see themselves as gangsters or gentlemen thieves. They devour forbidden books, delight in avant-garde literature in which revolutionary authors break boundaries and compose alexandrines which they call "tragedies."

Here are profound emotional conflicts. Here is a new "Triangle": the husband, the wife, and the lover.

A Spanish prince is torn between loyalty to his father and his mistress; a chauvinistic old man contemplates a fratricidal conflict between his three sons and their brothers-in-law. An incestuous queen is inflamed with passion for her chaste son-in-law.

These schoolchildren also delight in short stories known as fables, featuring animals of all kinds: the fox, the stork, the weasel, the rabbit, the cicada, and the ant.

As is to be expected, their teachers disdain such frivolous things. All the same, there is a chance that these hated tragedies and fables, with their disconcerting and outrageous novelty, might themselves become Classics one day....

# A PARTING MESSAGE
# TO THE READER

Dearest reader and friend, here ends the first series of enigmatic tales which I have copied out for you at the top of *la Tour Pointue*. I hope they have helped you to forget about your everyday concerns, like settling your butcher's bill, as well as the more serious problems of domestic and international politics, for a little while at least.

This is not goodbye but *adieu*, dearest reader and friend.

As soon as I am able, I will return to the mousetrap. Beneath the air vent, I will investigate the wall—the secret of which is now known to me. I will delicately place my index finger on the invisible button, venture through the narrow tunnel and up the staircase with ninety-three steps, and will again reach the top of la Tour Pointue.

Not all nights are moonlit; as a precaution, I will bring candles. And when I have more stories, you will be the first to know.

But above all, you must keep my secret! Think, dearest reader and friend—just imagine: if I were to be found out....

# EXPLANATORY NOTES

**Urbin's Chin**
**Paul Verlaine** (1844-1896)—*fin de siècle* symbolist poet and contemporary of Arthur Rimbaud. His distinctive appearance can be seen in numerous photographs.

**Police Technique**
**Tennis like Borotra**—reference to Jean Borotra (1898-1994), the "Bounding Basque" who won Wimbledon in 1924 and 1926, the Australian championship in 1928, and the French title in 1924 and 1931.

**Swam like Taris**—reference to Jean Taris (1909-1977), Olympic swimmer and subject of Jean Vigo's pioneering 1931 short film, *Taris, champion de natation* (Jean Taris, Swimming Champion).

**Drove like Chiron**—reference to Louis Chiron (1899-1979), five-time winner of the French Grand Prix. The Bugatti Chiron, a luxury sports car, is named in his honor.

**Prosper Lepicq**—Véry 's series detective, Lepicq is a lawyer and amateur sleuth who appears in seven novels. These are:
*Meurtre au quai des Orfèvres* (1934)
*M. Marcel des Pompes funèbres* (1934)
**L'Assassinat du Père Noël** (1934)
*Le Réglo* (1935)
*Les Disparus de Saint-Agil* (1935)
*Le Gentleman des antipodes* (1936)
*Le Thé des vieilles dames* (1937)

**The Disappearance of Emmeline Poke**
**Radiesthesia**—a pseudoscience often used synonymously with "dowsing" or "divining."

**The Tale of a Tartlet** (Originally published as "Police Montée.")
**Kilini's Reaction**—appears to be a reference to the Kiliani-Fischer synthesis, which is named in honor of German chemists

149

Heinrich Kiliani and Nobel Prize winner Emil Fischer. The term refers to a process for synthesizing simple sugars, or monosaccharides. Kiliani also lent his name to the "Kiliani-Nomenklatur," a means of notating chemical reactions which was in relatively common usage in the early decades of the twentieth century, but has since fallen out of favor. It has been posited elsewhere that glucose is a reactive counteragent to cyanide, though this has not been conclusively proven. Needless to say, it is strongly advised that you do not try this experiment, or anything like it, for yourself.

**Bougault & Perrier**—a reference to J. Bougault and J. Perrier, whose quantitative research into "the action of hydrocyanic acid on glucose" and "Kiliani's reaction" was recorded by the French Academy of Sciences on May 17th, 1920 and cited in numerous scientific journals thereafter. (Nature, June 3rd, 1920)

**Saint-Rat**—a reference to Louis de Saint-Rat, who was Head of Biological Chemistry at the Sorbonne between 1922 and 1957, and an important figure in public health, sanitation and food hygiene. Among his honors were the *Légion d'Honneur, l'Ordre de Leopold* and *l'Ordre du Mérite pour la Recherche et l'Invention.*

**The Salvation of Maxim Zapyrov** (Originally published as "La Multiplication des Nègres")

The "Bal Nègre"—The "Negro Ball" was a nickname given to *Le Bal Colonial* dance hall, a nightspot which catered largely to Black Parisians.

**The Spanish Prisoner**

The *Bottin Mondain*—a French social directory akin to Who's Who, first published in 1903.

**The "Spanish prisoner" scam**—a famous confidence trick chronicled notably in the memoirs of influential criminologist Eugène Vidocq. Typically the (non-existent) Spanish prisoner is a person of considerable wealth, wrongly imprisoned. The "mark" (target for the scam) is entreated to donate a sum of money with a promise of a more substantial monetary reward once the prisoner has been freed. Needless to say, the reward is not forthcoming, and once the initial donation has been made, the Spanish prisoner is never heard from again.

**A Lesson in Crime** (Originally published in a slightly different form as "A quand des cours de littérature criminelle?" in *Marianne, grand hebdomadaire littéraire illustré*, volume 3, issue 120, February 6th, 1935.)

**Mademoiselle Stangerson, Joseph Rouletabille and Frederic Larsan**—all main characters in one of France's greatest mystery novels, and one which is discussed at length elsewhere in *The Pointed Tower: The Mystery of the Yellow Room* by Gaston Leroux.

*The Lerouge Affair*—published in 1866, this is often described as the first French detective story. In it, author Emile Gaboriau introduces his celebrated fictional police detective Monsieur Lecoq (inspired by the real-life Eugène Vidocq) and the bed-bound sleuth Tabaret.

*The Hollow Needle*—serialized between November 1908 and May 1909, this is the first full-length novel to feature Maurice Leblanc's gentleman thief, Arsène Lupin. The titular needle refers to a pointed rock formation at Étretat, as depicted in impressionist Claude Monet's 1885 piece, "Étretat, the Needle Rock and Porte d'Aval."

*The Murder of Roger Ackroyd*—first published in 1926, this is one of the most celebrated outings of Agatha Christie's world-famous sleuth, Hercule Poirot.

*The Lament of Fualdès*—a reference to the murder of French magistrate Antoine Fualdès, whose body was found floating in the Aveyron river in 1817.

**The Lament of Troppmann**—a reference to Jean-Baptiste Troppmann, who murdered six children and two adults in the summer of 1869, and who was guillotined in January 1870. His execution was vividly chronicled by Ivan Turgenev in "The Execution of Troppmann": ("something suddenly descended with a hollow growl and stopped with an abrupt thud... just as though a huge animal had retched [...] immediately after the execution, as the body, which had been thrown into the van, was rapidly being taken away, two men [forced] their way through the lines of soldiers, and crawling under the guillotine, they began wetting their handkerchiefs in the blood that had dripped through the chinks of the planks...").

**The Lament of Landru**—Landru should need no introduction to readers of this book. Nonetheless: Henri Landru, known as the "Bluebeard of Gambais," was a serial killer and confidence trickster convicted of eleven murders between 1915 and 1919—though it is believed that he actually killed many more.

**Violette Nozière**—The notorious Violette memorably portrayed by Isabelle Huppert in Claude Chabrol's 1978 film of the same name. In 1933, at the age of 18, she murdered her father with rat poison and attempted to murder her mother. She was subsequently convicted and sentenced to death, though she was eventually released from prison in 1945, dying in obscurity in 1966.

**Vidocq**—A reference to the aforementioned Eugène Vidocq, criminal turned criminologist and private detective who in 1811 formed France's first police force: the Brigade de Sûreté.

**The Inexplicable Gallery**—a reference to chapter seventeen of The Mystery of the Yellow Room.

**Odeur Funèbre**—a reference to Véry 's own 1934 novel *Les quatre vipères*.

**Lupin's monologue in the fifth act of 813**—a reference to 813, the second of Maurice Leblanc's novels featuring Arsène Lupin, in which Lupin finds himself falsely accused of three murders and must prove his innocence.

## THE SECRET OF THE POINTED TOWER

*THE SECRET OF The Pointed Tower* by Pierrre Very is printed on 60-pound paper, and is designed by Jeffrey Marks using InDesign. The type is PSFournier, a font named for French engraver Pierre Simo Fournier. The cover is by Joshua Luboski. The first edition was published in a perfect-bound softcover edition. *The Secret Of The Pointed Tower* was printed by Southern Ohio Printers and bound by Cincinnati Bindery. The book was published in October 2023 by Crippen & Landru Publishers.

Crippen & Landru, Publishers

P. O. Box 532057

Cincinnati, OH 45253

Web: www.Crippenlandru.com

E-mail: orders@crippenlandru.com

SINCE 1994, CRIPPEN & Landru has published more than 100 first editions of short-story collections by important detective and mystery writers.

*This is the best edited, most attractively packaged line of mystery books introduced in this decade. The books are equally valuable to collectors and readers.* [Mystery Scene Magazine]

*The specialty publisher with the most star-studded list is Crippen & Landru, which has produced short story collections by some of the biggest names in contemporary crime fiction.* [Ellery Queen's Mystery Magazine]

*God bless Crippen & Landru.* [The Strand Magazine]

*A monument in the making is appearing year by year from Crippen & Landru, a small press devoted exclusively to publishing the criminous short story.* [Alfred Hitchcock's Mystery Magazine]

# Crippen & Landru
# Lost Classics

Peter Godfrey. *The Newtonian Egg*. 2002.

Craig Rice. *Murder, Mystery, and Malone*. 2002 eBook, $8.99

Charles B. Child. *The Sleuth of Baghdad*. 2002.

Stuart Palmer. *Hildegarde Withers, Uncollected Riddles*. 2002 eBook $8.99

Christianna Brand. *The Spotted Cat*. 2002

Raoul Whitfield. *Jo Gar's Casebook*. 2002.

William Campbell Gault. *Marksman*. 2003.

Gerald Kersh. *Karmesin*. 2003 eBook, $8.99

C. Daly King. *The Complete Curious Mr. Tarrant*. 2003 eBook $8.99

Helen McCloy. *The Pleasant Assassin*. 2003

William DeAndrea. *Murder – All Kinds*. 2003

Anthony Berkeley. *The Avenging Chance*. 2004

Joseph Commings. *Banner Deadlines*. 2004 eBook $8.99

Erle Stanley Gardner. *The Danger Zone*. 2004 eBook $8.99

T. S. Stribling. *Dr. Poggioli: Criminologist*. 2004 eBook $8.99

Margaret Millar. *The Couple Next Door*. 2004

Gladys Mitchell. *Sleuth's Alchemy*. 2005

Philip Warne/Howard Macy. *Who Was Guilty?* 2005 eBook $8.99

Dennis Lynds writing as Michael Collins. *Slot-Machine Kelly*. 2005

Julian Symons. *The Detections of Francis Quarles*. 2006

Rafael Sabatini. *The Evidence of the Sword*. 2006 eBook, $8.99

Erle Stanley Gardner. *The Casebook of Sidney Zoom*. 2006, eBook $8.99

Ellis Peters. *The Trinity Cat*. 2006

Lloyd Biggle. *The Grandfather Rastin Mysteries*. 2007

Max Brand. *Masquerade*. 2007

Mignon Eberhart. *Dead Yesterday*. 2007

Hugh Pentecost. *The Battles of Jericho*. 2008

Victor Canning. *The Minerva Club*. 2009

Anthony Boucher and Denis Green. *The Casebook of Gregory Hood*. 2009

Vera Caspary. *The Murder in the Stork Club*. 2009

Michael Innes. *Appleby Talks About Crime*. 2010

Phillip Wylie. *Ten Thousand Blunt Instruments*. 2010

Erle Stanley Gardner. *The Exploits of the Patent Leather Kid*. 2010, eBook, $8.99

Vincent Cornier. *The Duel of Shadows*. 2011, eBook, $8.99

E. X. Ferrars. *The Casebook of Jonas P. Jonas*. 2012

Charlotte Armstrong. *Night Call*. 2014, eBook, $8.99

Phyllis Bentley. *Chain of Witnesses*. 2014

Patrick Quentin. *The Puzzles of Peter Duluth*. 2016, , Clothbound $29, eBook $8.99

Frederick Irving Anderson . *The Purple Flame*. 2016, Clothbound $29, Trade Paperback $19

Anthony Gilbert. *Sequel to Murder*. 2017, Clothbound $29

James Holding, *The Zanzibar Shirt Mystery*. 2018, Clothbound $29

Q. Patrick. *The Cases of Lieutenant Trant*. 2019

Erle Stanley Gardner. *Hot Cash, Cold Clews*. 2020, Clothbound $32, Trade Paperback $22, eBook $8.99

Freeman Wills Crofts, *The 9.50 Up Express*. 2021, Clothbound $32, Trade Paperback $22, eBook $8.99

Stuart Palmer. *Hildegarde Withers, Final Riddles?* 2021, Clothbound $32, Trade Paperback $22, eBook $8.99

Patrick Quentin. *Hunt in the Dark*. 2021

William Brittain. *The Man Who Solved Mysteries*. 2022, Clothbound $32, Trade Paperback $1922 eBook $8.99

John Creasey. *Gideon and the Young Toughs*. 2022, , Clothbound $35, Trade Paperback $20, eBook $8.99

Pierre Very. *The Secret of the Pointed Tower*. 2023, Clothbound $32, Trade Paperback $20

Anthony Berkeley. *The Avenging Chance and Even More Stories (Enlarged with Two Stories)*. 2023, Trade Paperback $19, eBook $8.99

## *Subscriptions*

SUBSCRIBERS AGREE TO purchase each forthcoming publication, either the Regular Series or the Lost Classics or (preferably) both. Collectors can thereby guarantee receiving limited editions, and readers won't miss any favorite stories.

Subscribers receive a discount of 20% off the list price (and the same discount on our backlist) and a specially commissioned short story by a major writer in a deluxe edition as a gift at the end of the year.

The point for us is that, since customers don't pick and choose which books they want, we have a guaranteed sale even before the book is published, and that allows us to be more imaginative in choosing short story collections to issue.

That's worth the 20% discount for us. Sign up now and start saving. Email us at orders@crippenlandru.com or visit our website at www.crippenlandru.com on our subscription page.